#3 On the Case with Holmes and Watson

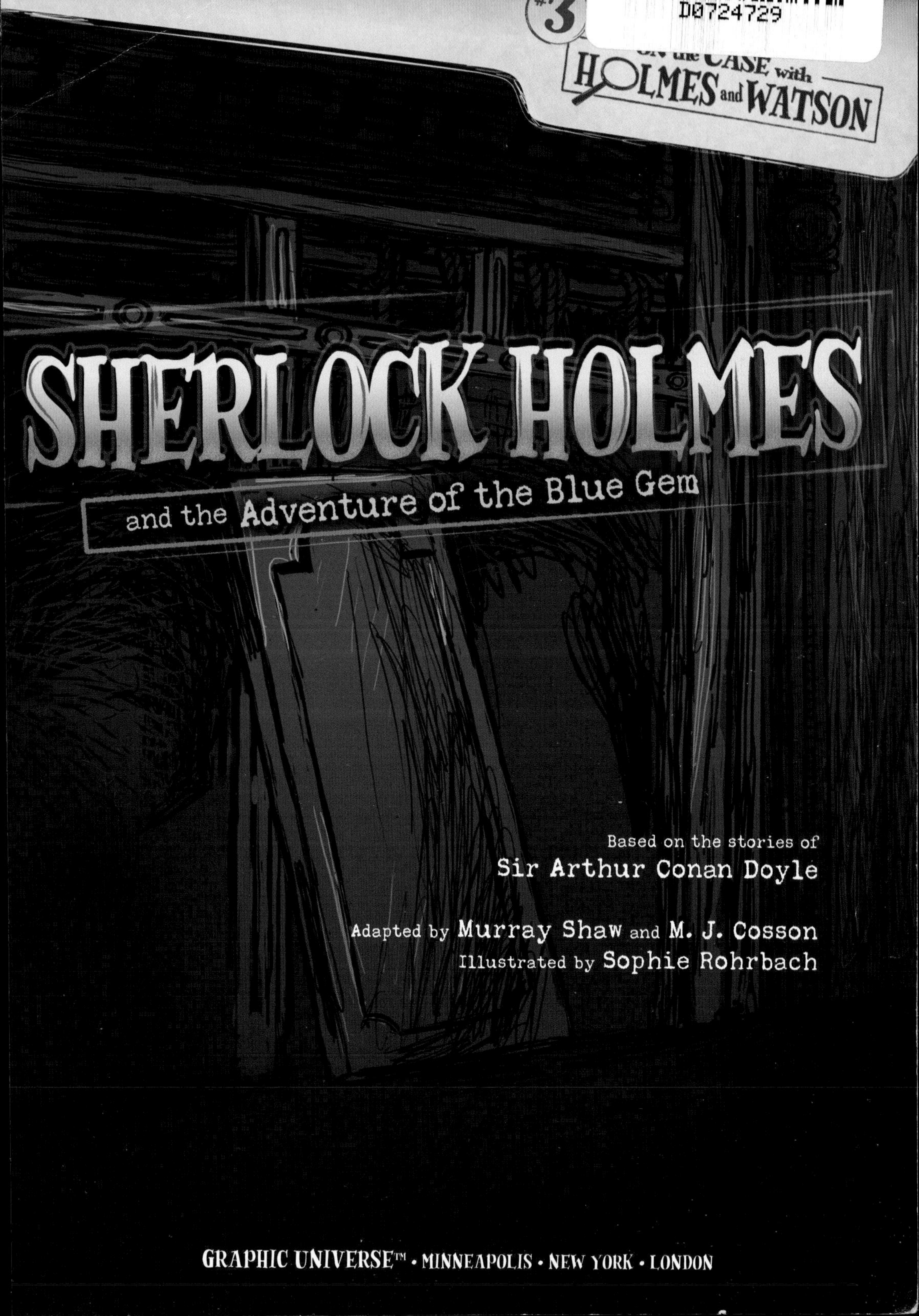

SHERLOCK HOLMES

and the Adventure of the Blue Gem

Based on the stories of
Sir Arthur Conan Doyle

Adapted by Murray Shaw and M. J. Cosson
Illustrated by Sophie Rohrbach

GRAPHIC UNIVERSE™ • MINNEAPOLIS • NEW YORK • LONDON

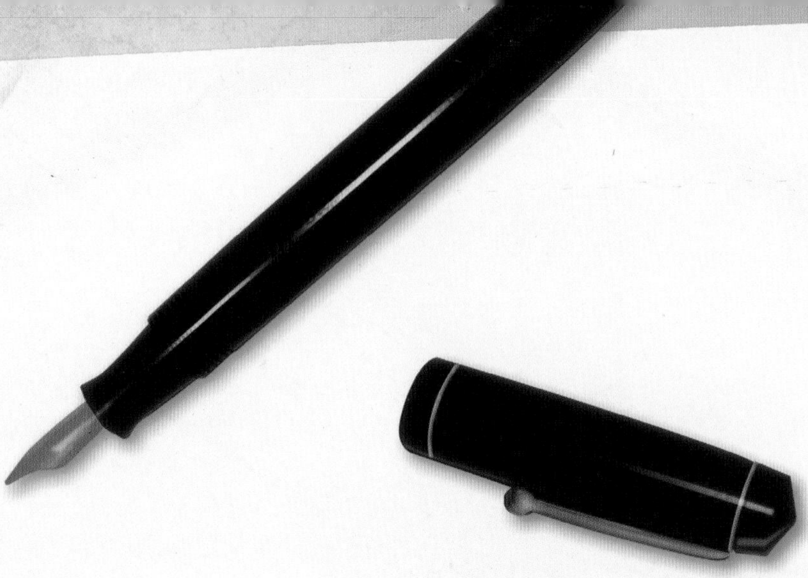

Grateful acknowledgment to Dame Jean Conan Doyle for permission to use the
Sherlock Holmes characters created by Sir Arthur Conan Doyle

Graphic Universe™
A division of Lerner Publishing Group, Inc.
241 First Avenue North
Minneapolis, MN 55401 U.S.A.

Website address: www.lernerbooks.com

Library of Congress Cataloging-in-Publication Data

Shaw, Murray.
     #3 Sherlock Holmes and the adventure of the blue gem / adapted by
Murray Shaw and M.J. Cosson ; illustrated by Sophie Rohrbach ; from the
original stories by Sir Arthur Conan Doyle.
     p.   cm. — (On the case with Holmes and Watson)
     Summary: Retold in graphic novel form, Sherlock Holmes investigates
how an exquisite blue gem came to be in the throat of a Christmas goose.
Includes a section explaining Holmes's reasoning and the clues he used to
solve the mystery.
     ISBN 978-0-7613-6190-9 (lib. bdg. : alk. paper)
     I. Graphic novels. (I. Graphic novels. 2. Doyle, Arthur Conan, Sir,
1859-1930. Adventure of the blue carbuncle—Adaptations. 3. Mystery and
detective stories.) I. Cosson, M. J. II. Rohrbach, Sophie, ill. III. Doyle,
Arthur Conan, Sir, 1859-1930. Adventure of the blue carbuncle. IV. Title.
V. Title: Adventure of the blue gem.
PZ7.7.S46Shi 2011   2009051758
741.5'973—dc22

Manufactured in the United States of America
1—CG—7/15/10

The Story of
SHERLOCK HOLMES
The Famous Detective

Sherlock Holmes and his helpful friend Dr. John Watson are fictional characters created by British writer Sir Arthur Conan Doyle. Doyle published his first novel about the pair, *A Study in Scarlet*, in 1887, and it became very successful. Doyle went on to write fifty-six short stories, as well as three more novels about Holmes's adventures—*The Sign of Four* (1890), *The Hound of the Baskervilles* (1902), and *The Valley of Fear* (1915).

Sherlock Holmes and Dr. Watson have become some of the most famous book characters of all time. Holmes spent most of his time solving mysteries, but he also had a wide array of hobbies, such as playing the violin, boxing, and sword fighting. Watson, a retired army doctor, met Holmes through a mutual friend when Holmes was looking for a roommate. Watson lived with Holmes for several years at 221B Baker Street before marrying and moving out. However, after his marriage, Watson continued to assist Holmes with his cases.

The original versions of the Sherlock Holmes stories are still printed, and many have been made into movies and television shows. Readers continue to be impressed by Holmes's detective methods of observation and scientific reason.

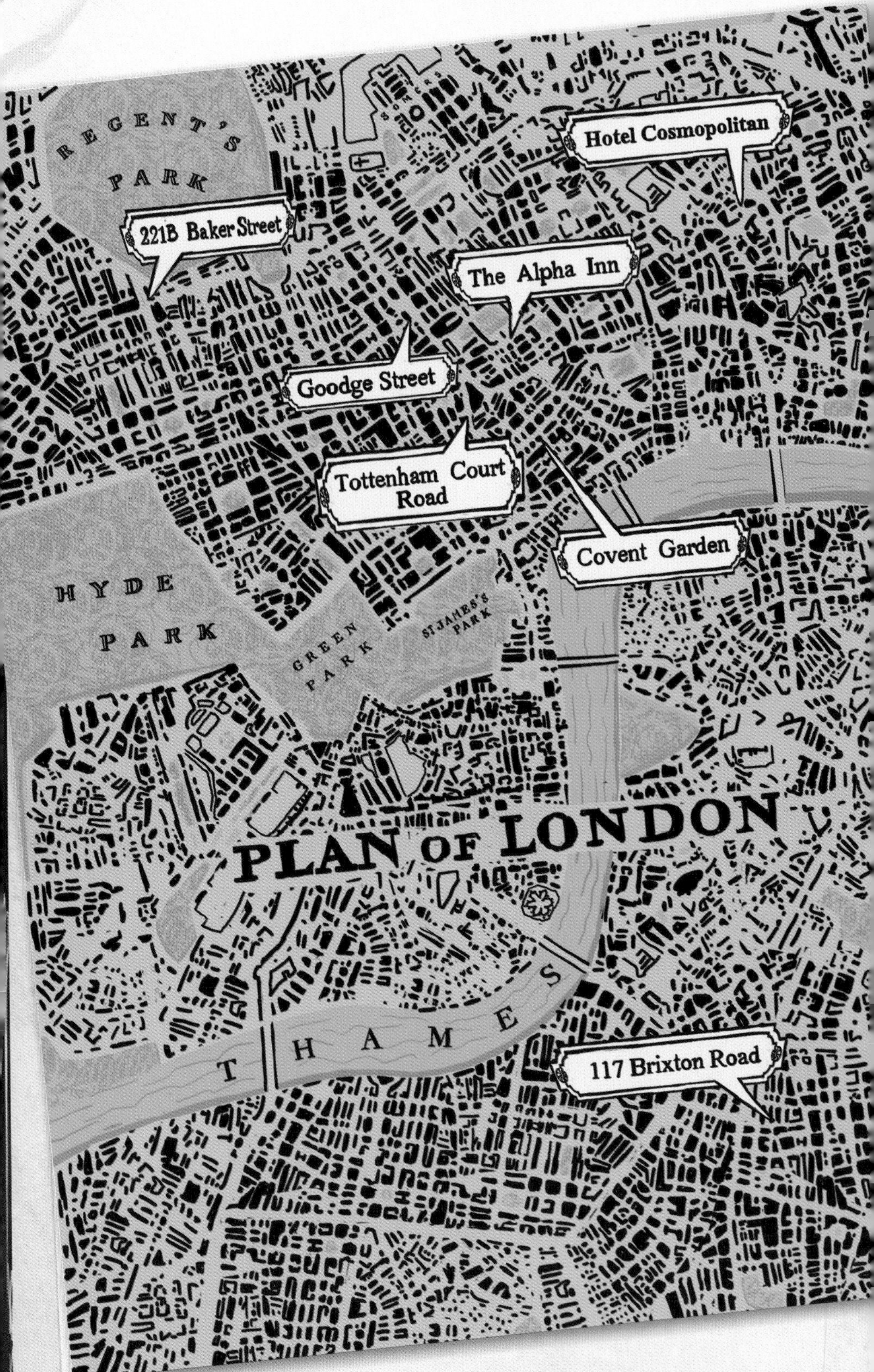
REGENT'S PARK
221B Baker Street
Hotel Cosmopolitan
The Alpha Inn
Goodge Street
Tottenham Court Road
Covent Garden
HYDE PARK
GREEN PARK
ST JAMES'S PARK
PLAN OF LONDON
THAMES
117 Brixton Road

Character List

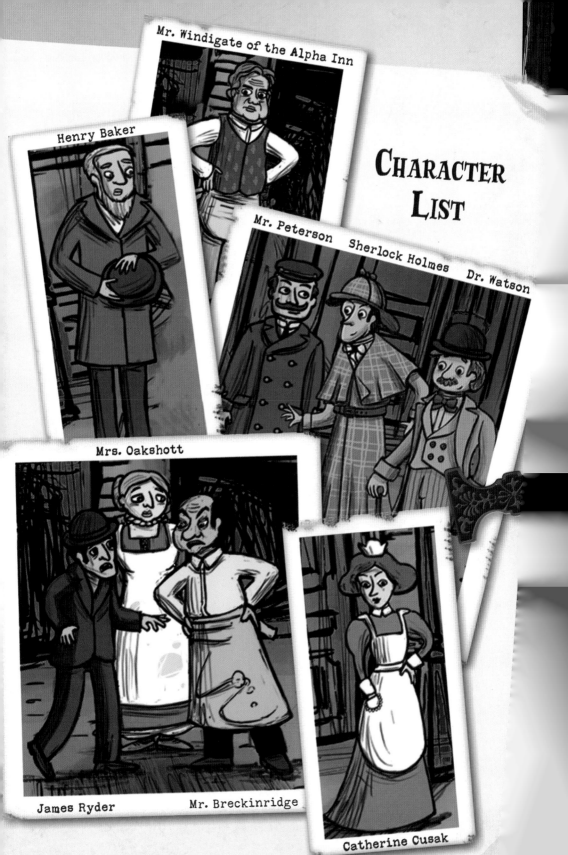

Mr. Windigate of the Alpha Inn

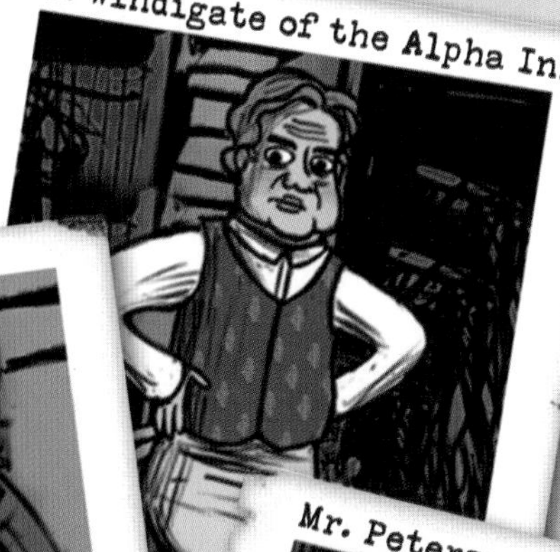

Henry Baker

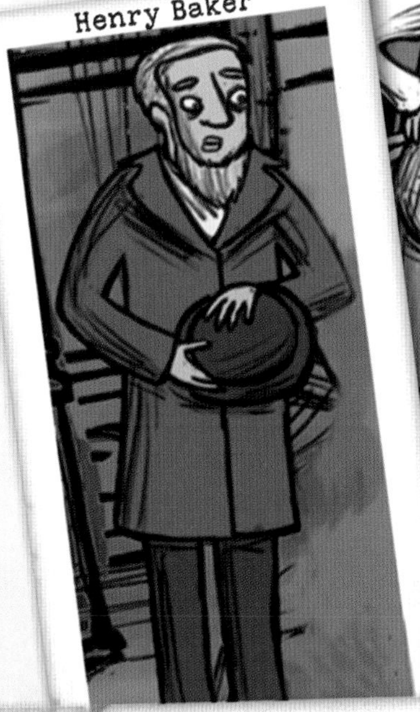

Mr. Peterson Sherlock Holmes Dr. Watson

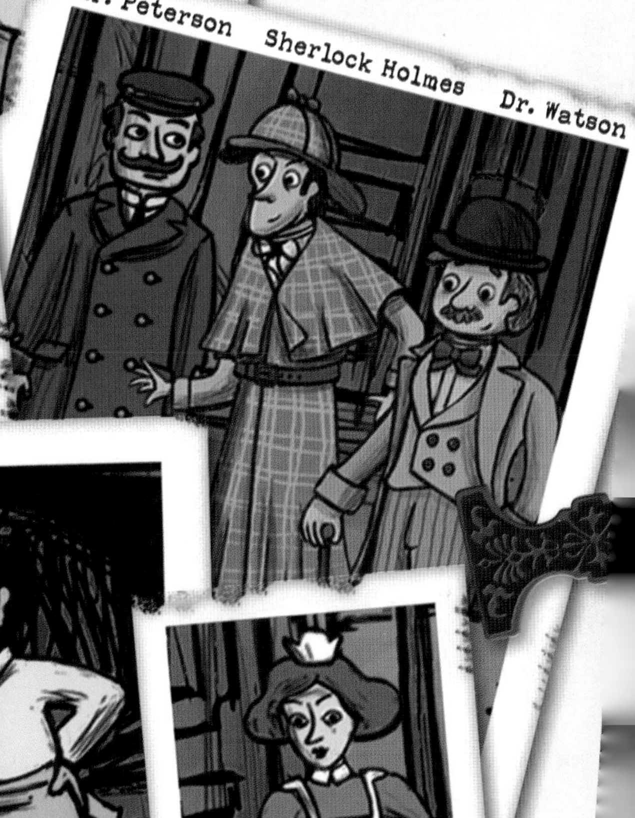

Mrs. Oakshott

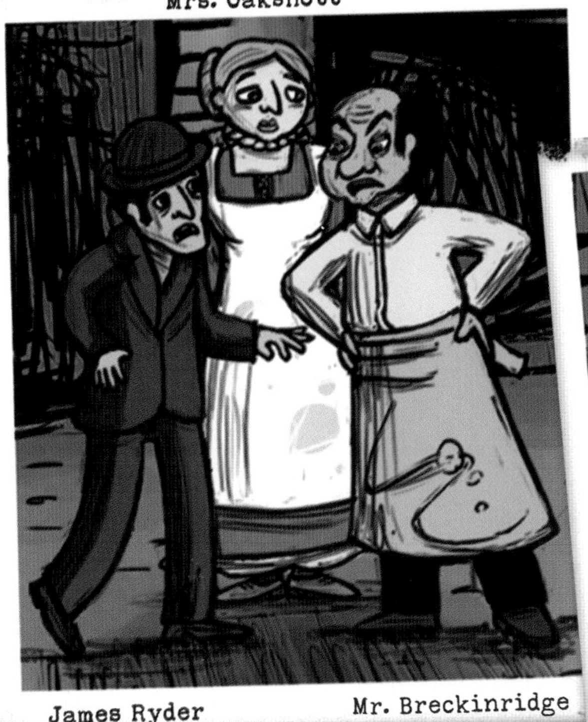

James Ryder Mr. Breckinridge

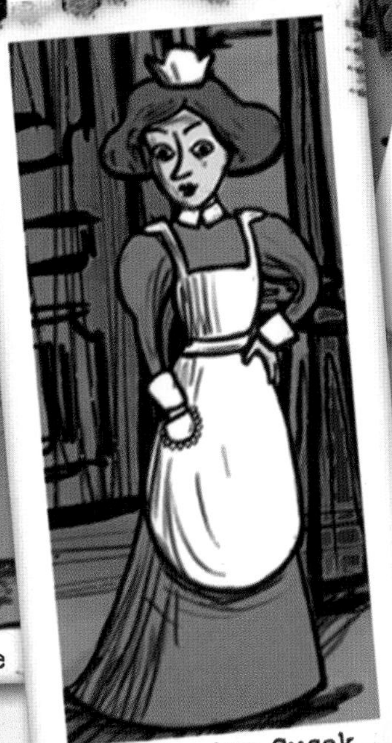

Catherine Cusak

From the Desk of
John H. Watson, M.D.

My name is Dr. John H. Watson. For several years, I have been assisting my friend, Sherlock Holmes, in solving mysteries throughout the bustling city of London and beyond. Holmes is a peculiar man—always questioning and reasoning his way through various problems. But when I first met him in 1878, I was immediately intrigued by his oddities.

Holmes has always been more daring than I, and his logical deduction never ceases to amaze me. I have begun writing down all of the adventures I have with Holmes. This is one of those stories.

Sincerely,

Dr. Watson

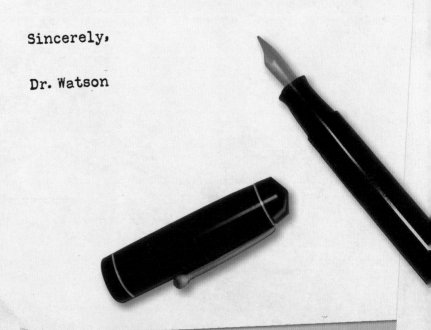

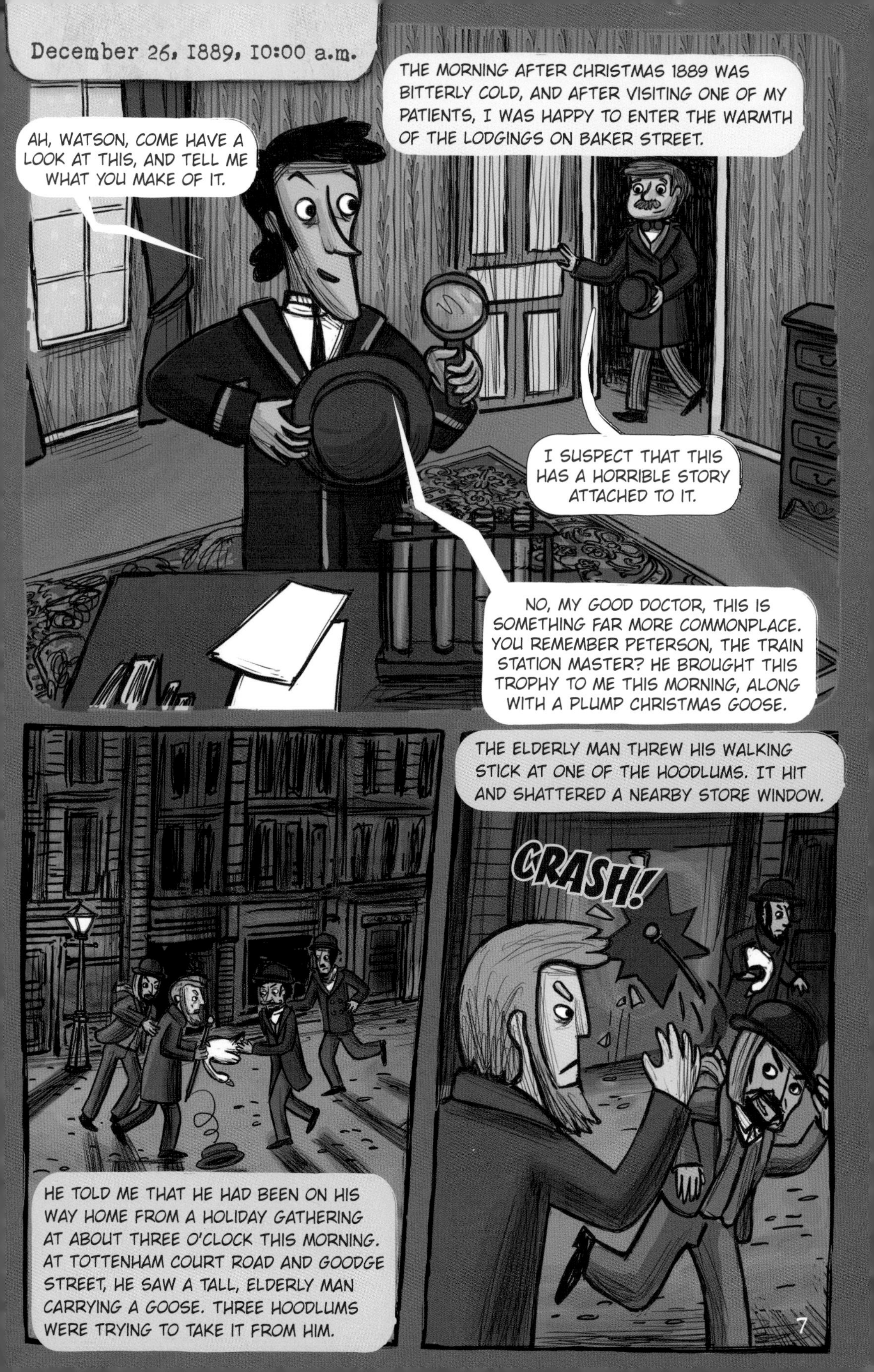
December 26, 1889, 10:00 a.m.
THE MORNING AFTER CHRISTMAS 1889 WAS BITTERLY COLD, AND AFTER VISITING ONE OF MY PATIENTS, I WAS HAPPY TO ENTER THE WARMTH OF THE LODGINGS ON BAKER STREET.
AH, WATSON, COME HAVE A LOOK AT THIS, AND TELL ME WHAT YOU MAKE OF IT.
I SUSPECT THAT THIS HAS A HORRIBLE STORY ATTACHED TO IT.
NO, MY GOOD DOCTOR, THIS IS SOMETHING FAR MORE COMMONPLACE. YOU REMEMBER PETERSON, THE TRAIN STATION MASTER? HE BROUGHT THIS TROPHY TO ME THIS MORNING, ALONG WITH A PLUMP CHRISTMAS GOOSE.
HE TOLD ME THAT HE HAD BEEN ON HIS WAY HOME FROM A HOLIDAY GATHERING AT ABOUT THREE O'CLOCK THIS MORNING. AT TOTTENHAM COURT ROAD AND GOODGE STREET, HE SAW A TALL, ELDERLY MAN CARRYING A GOOSE. THREE HOODLUMS WERE TRYING TO TAKE IT FROM HIM.
THE ELDERLY MAN THREW HIS WALKING STICK AT ONE OF THE HOODLUMS. IT HIT AND SHATTERED A NEARBY STORE WINDOW.
CRASH!

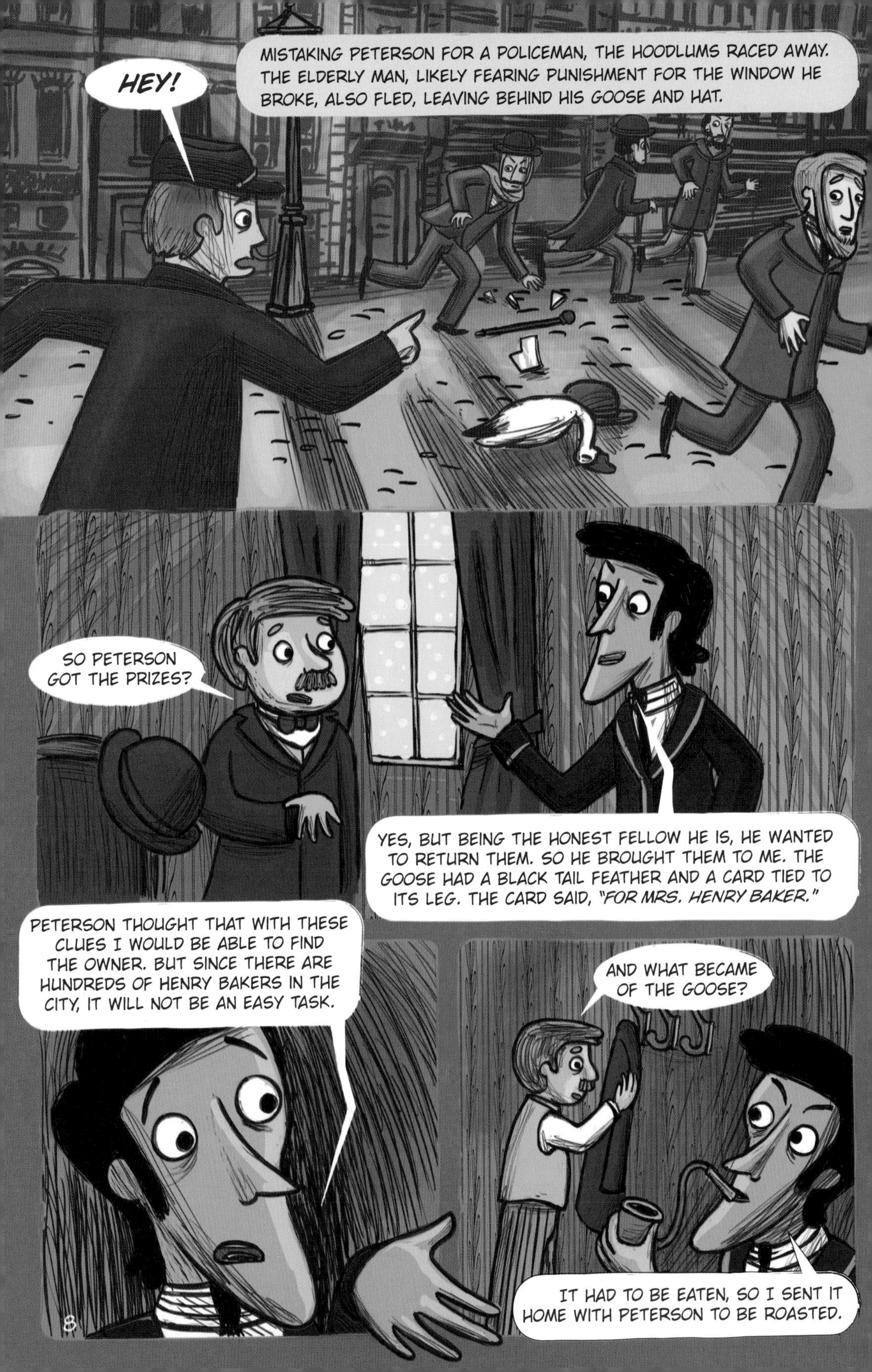

HEY!
MISTAKING PETERSON FOR A POLICEMAN, THE HOODLUMS RACED AWAY. THE ELDERLY MAN, LIKELY FEARING PUNISHMENT FOR THE WINDOW HE BROKE, ALSO FLED, LEAVING BEHIND HIS GOOSE AND HAT.
SO PETERSON GOT THE PRIZES?
YES, BUT BEING THE HONEST FELLOW HE IS, HE WANTED TO RETURN THEM. SO HE BROUGHT THEM TO ME. THE GOOSE HAD A BLACK TAIL FEATHER AND A CARD TIED TO ITS LEG. THE CARD SAID, *"FOR MRS. HENRY BAKER."*
PETERSON THOUGHT THAT WITH THESE CLUES I WOULD BE ABLE TO FIND THE OWNER. BUT SINCE THERE ARE HUNDREDS OF HENRY BAKERS IN THE CITY, IT WILL NOT BE AN EASY TASK.
AND WHAT BECAME OF THE GOOSE?
IT HAD TO BE EATEN, SO I SENT IT HOME WITH PETERSON TO BE ROASTED.

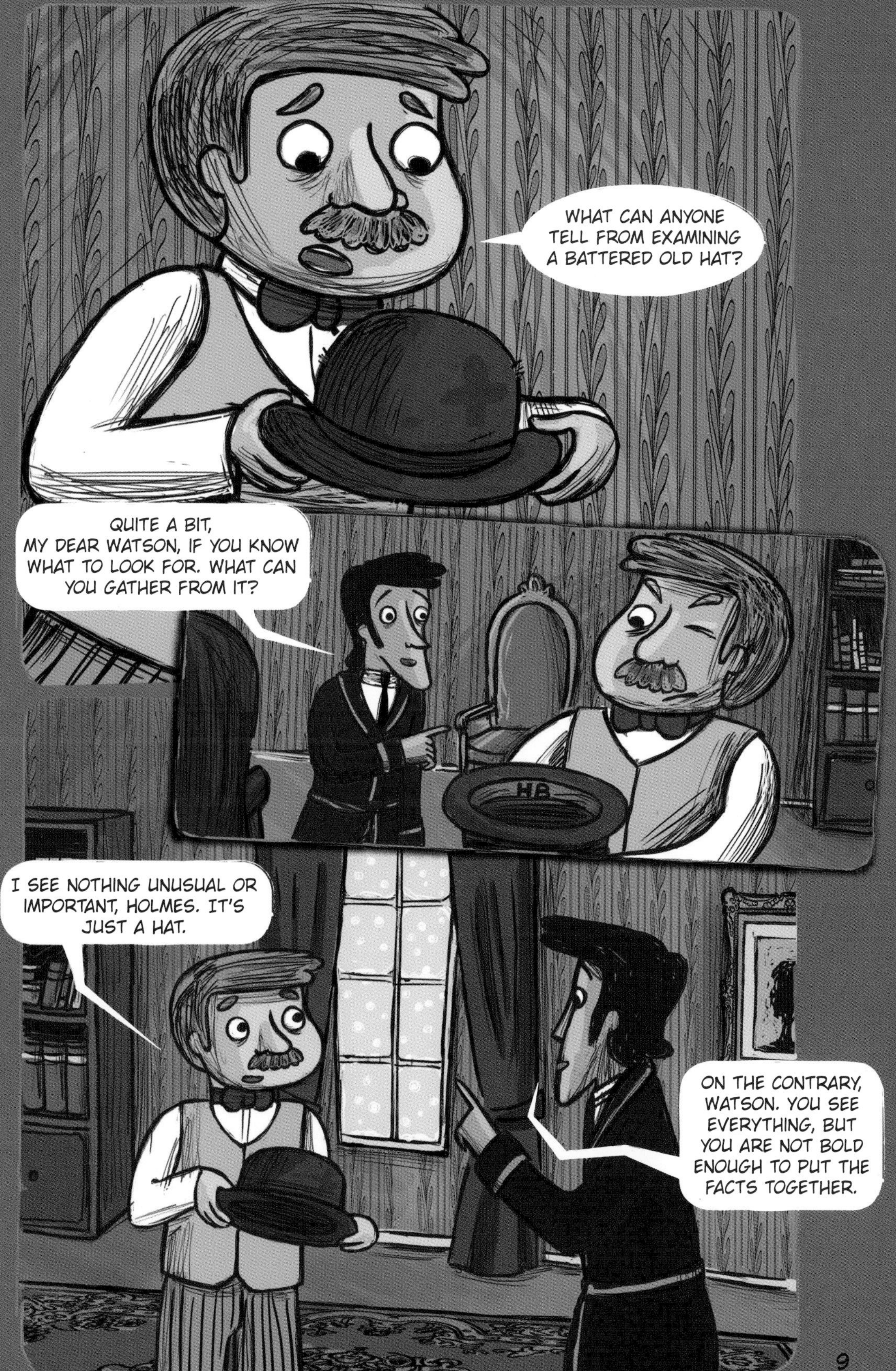

WHAT CAN ANYONE TELL FROM EXAMINING A BATTERED OLD HAT?
QUITE A BIT, MY DEAR WATSON, IF YOU KNOW WHAT TO LOOK FOR. WHAT CAN YOU GATHER FROM IT?
HB
I SEE NOTHING UNUSUAL OR IMPORTANT, HOLMES. IT'S JUST A HAT.
ON THE CONTRARY, WATSON. YOU SEE EVERYTHING, BUT YOU ARE NOT BOLD ENOUGH TO PUT THE FACTS TOGETHER.

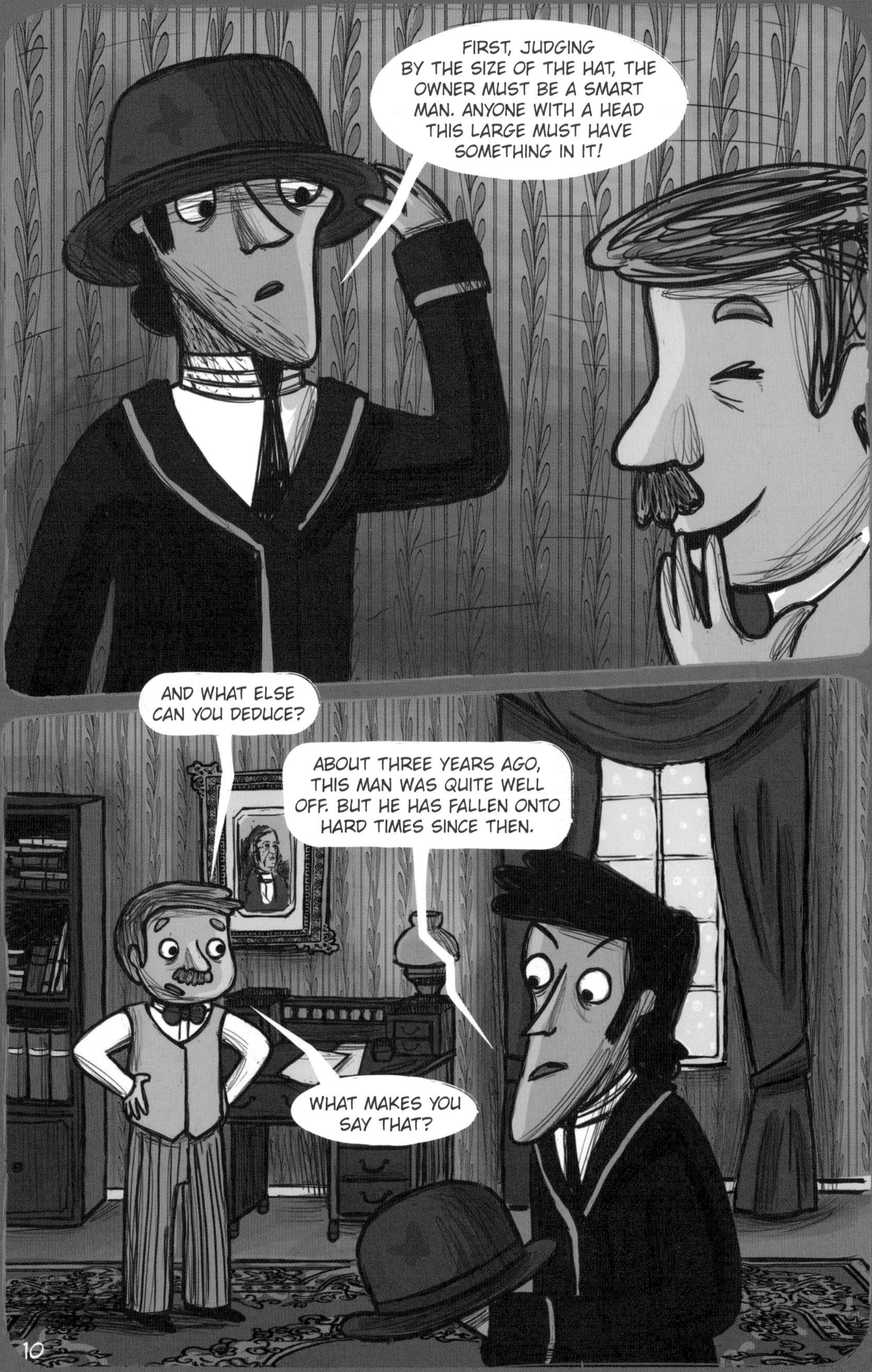
FIRST, JUDGING BY THE SIZE OF THE HAT, THE OWNER MUST BE A SMART MAN. ANYONE WITH A HEAD THIS LARGE MUST HAVE SOMETHING IN IT!
AND WHAT ELSE CAN YOU DEDUCE?
ABOUT THREE YEARS AGO, THIS MAN WAS QUITE WELL OFF. BUT HE HAS FALLEN ONTO HARD TIMES SINCE THEN.
WHAT MAKES YOU SAY THAT?

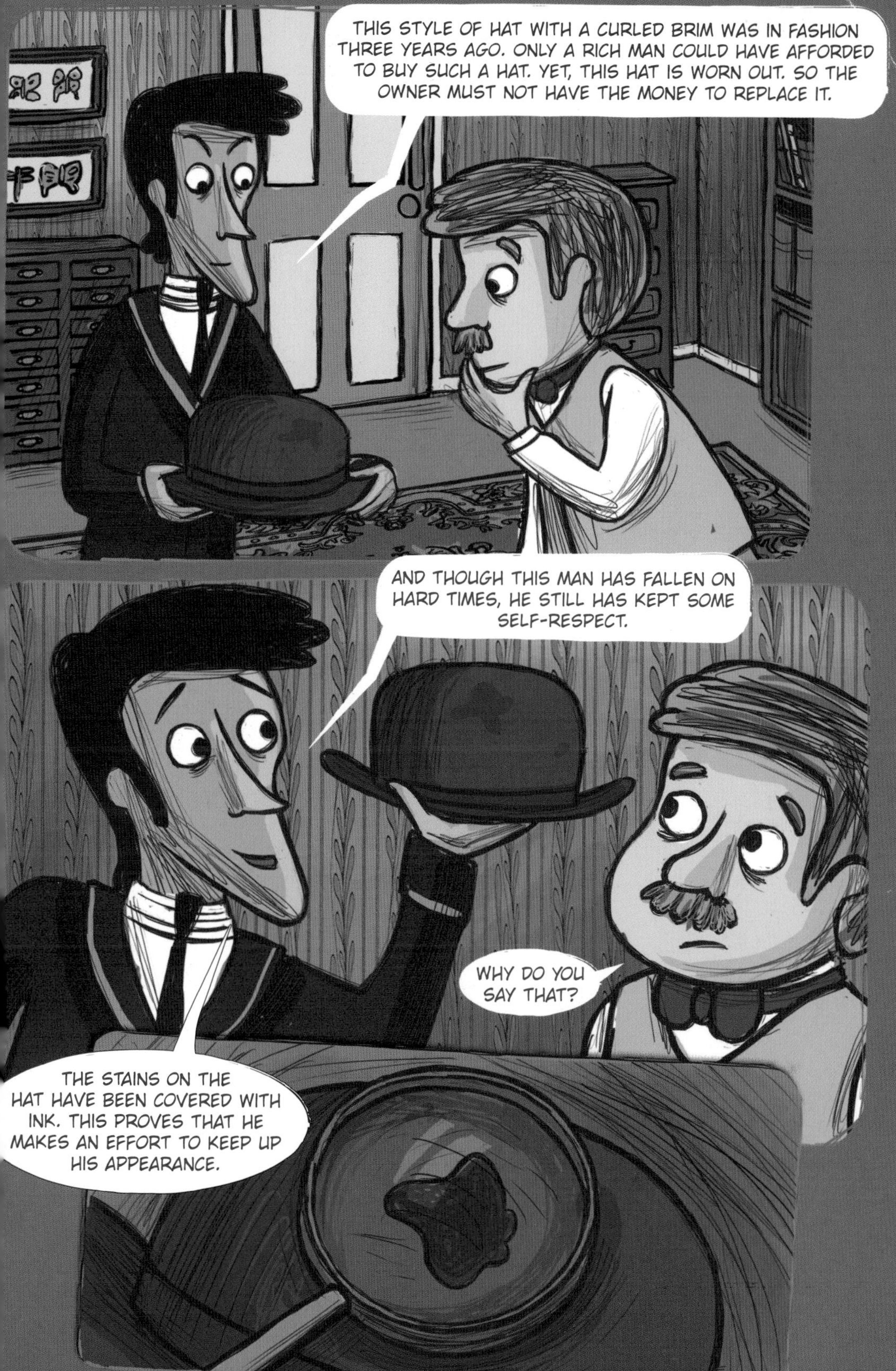
THIS STYLE OF HAT WITH A CURLED BRIM WAS IN FASHION THREE YEARS AGO. ONLY A RICH MAN COULD HAVE AFFORDED TO BUY SUCH A HAT. YET, THIS HAT IS WORN OUT. SO THE OWNER MUST NOT HAVE THE MONEY TO REPLACE IT.
AND THOUGH THIS MAN HAS FALLEN ON HARD TIMES, HE STILL HAS KEPT SOME SELF-RESPECT.
WHY DO YOU SAY THAT?
THE STAINS ON THE HAT HAVE BEEN COVERED WITH INK. THIS PROVES THAT HE MAKES AN EFFORT TO KEEP UP HIS APPEARANCE.

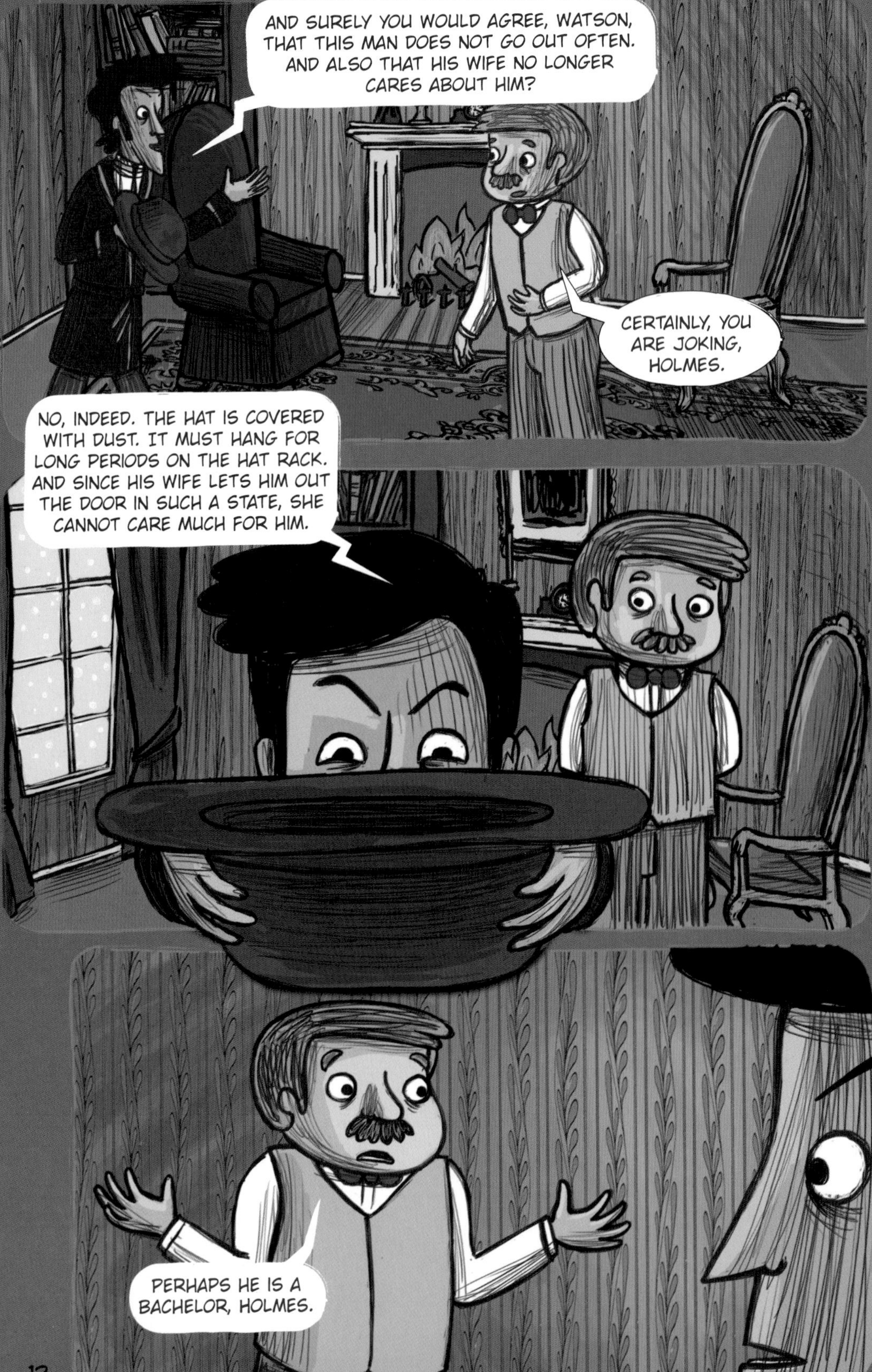
AND SURELY YOU WOULD AGREE, WATSON, THAT THIS MAN DOES NOT GO OUT OFTEN. AND ALSO THAT HIS WIFE NO LONGER CARES ABOUT HIM?
CERTAINLY, YOU ARE JOKING, HOLMES.
NO, INDEED. THE HAT IS COVERED WITH DUST. IT MUST HANG FOR LONG PERIODS ON THE HAT RACK. AND SINCE HIS WIFE LETS HIM OUT THE DOOR IN SUCH A STATE, SHE CANNOT CARE MUCH FOR HIM.
PERHAPS HE IS A BACHELOR, HOLMES.

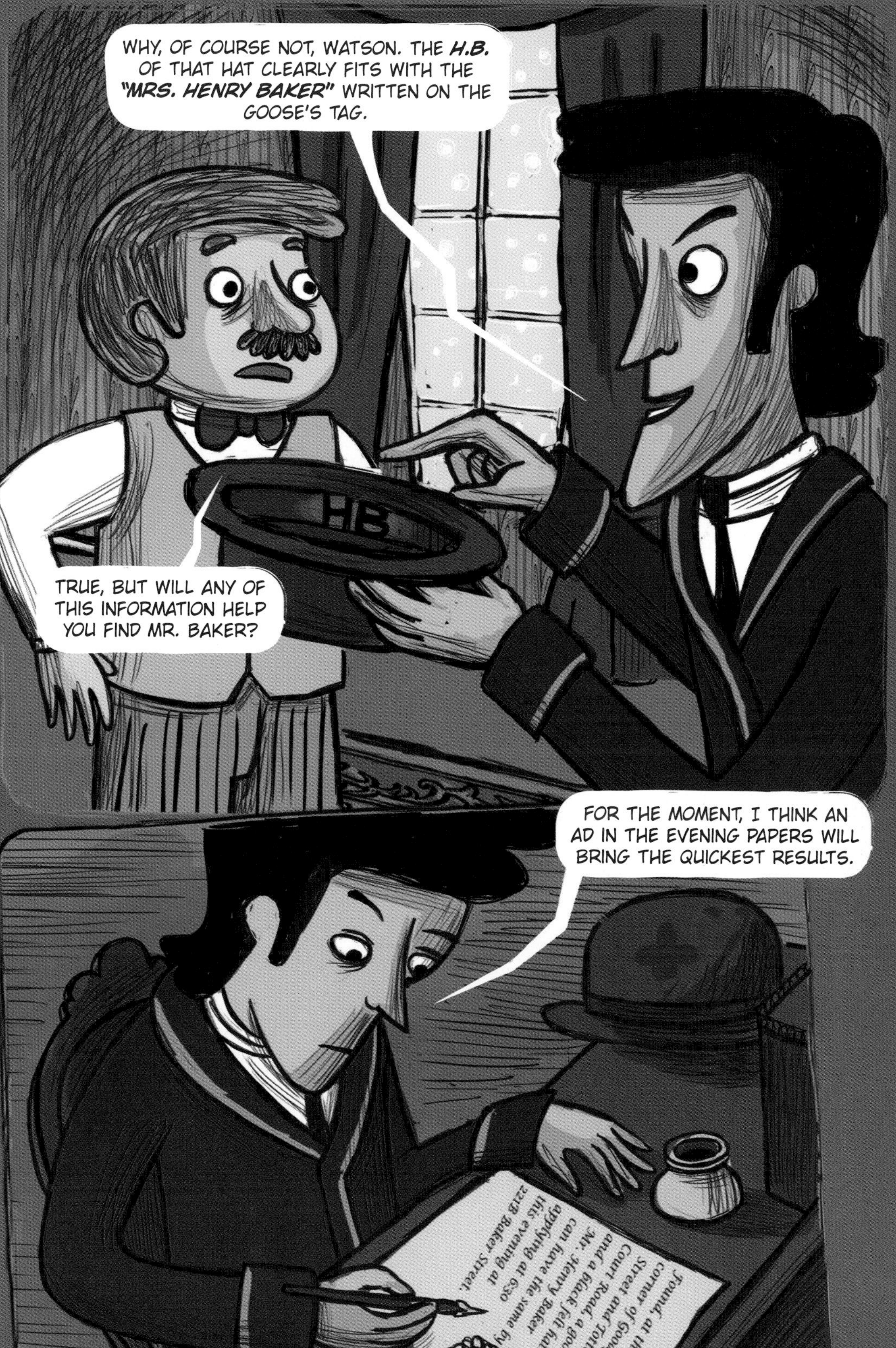
WHY, OF COURSE NOT, WATSON. THE *H.B.* OF THAT HAT CLEARLY FITS WITH THE *"MRS. HENRY BAKER"* WRITTEN ON THE GOOSE'S TAG.
HB
TRUE, BUT WILL ANY OF THIS INFORMATION HELP YOU FIND MR. BAKER?
FOR THE MOMENT, I THINK AN AD IN THE EVENING PAPERS WILL BRING THE QUICKEST RESULTS.
Found, at the corner of Goodge Street and Tottenham Court Road, a goose and a black felt hat. Mr. Henry Baker can have the same by applying at 6:30 this evening at 221B Baker Street.

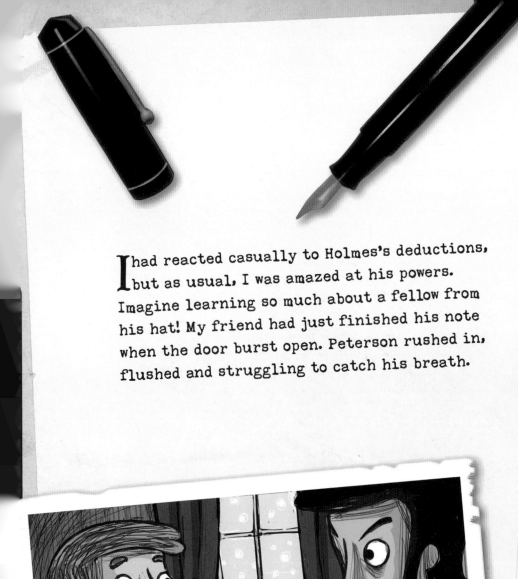

I had reacted casually to Holmes's deductions, but as usual, I was amazed at his powers. Imagine learning so much about a fellow from his hat! My friend had just finished his note when the door burst open. Peterson rushed in, flushed and struggling to catch his breath.

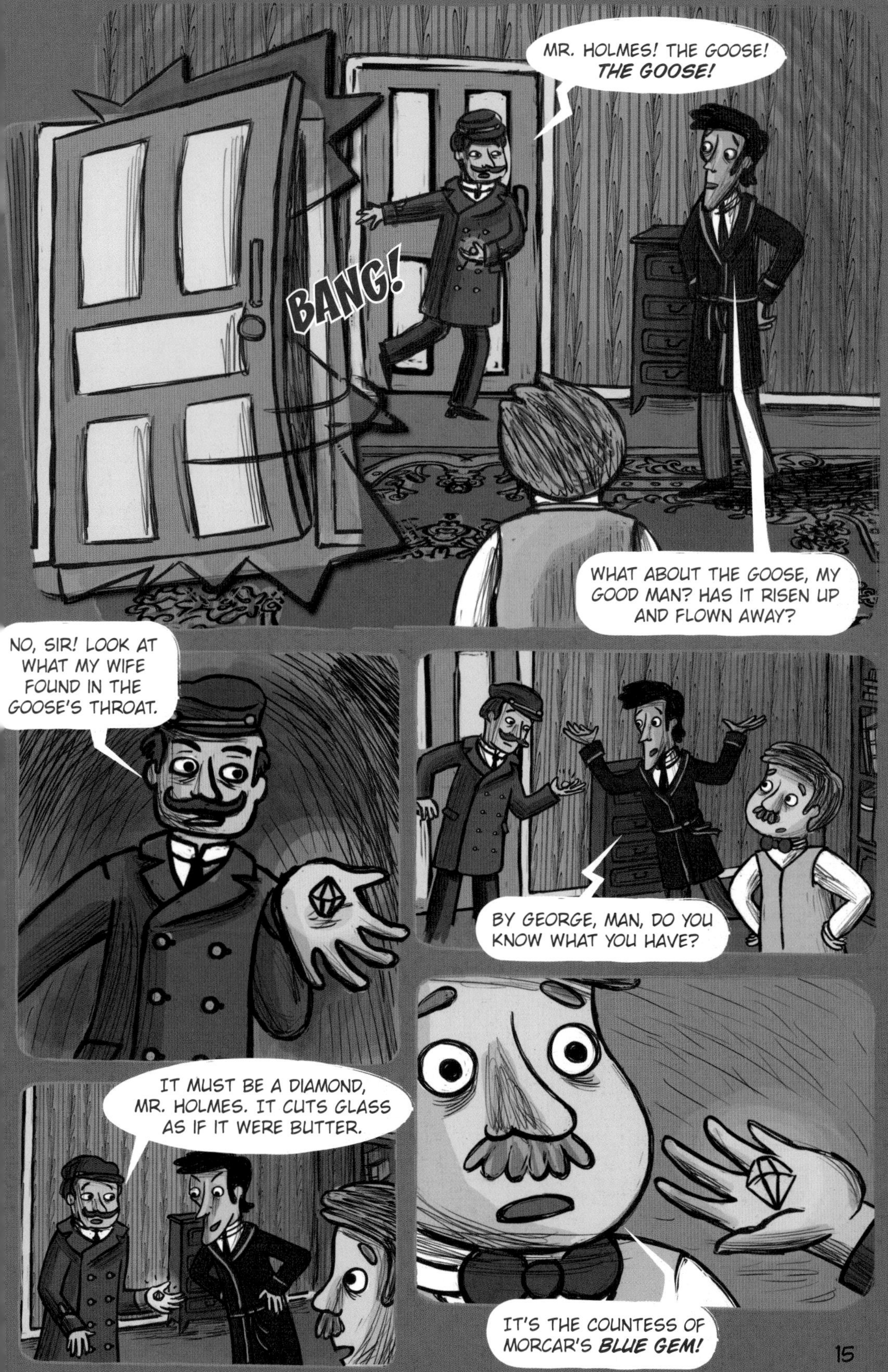
MR. HOLMES! THE GOOSE! ***THE GOOSE!***
BANG!
WHAT ABOUT THE GOOSE, MY GOOD MAN? HAS IT RISEN UP AND FLOWN AWAY?
NO, SIR! LOOK AT WHAT MY WIFE FOUND IN THE GOOSE'S THROAT.
BY GEORGE, MAN, DO YOU KNOW WHAT YOU HAVE?
IT MUST BE A DIAMOND, MR. HOLMES. IT CUTS GLASS AS IF IT WERE BUTTER.
IT'S THE COUNTESS OF MORCAR'S ***BLUE GEM!***

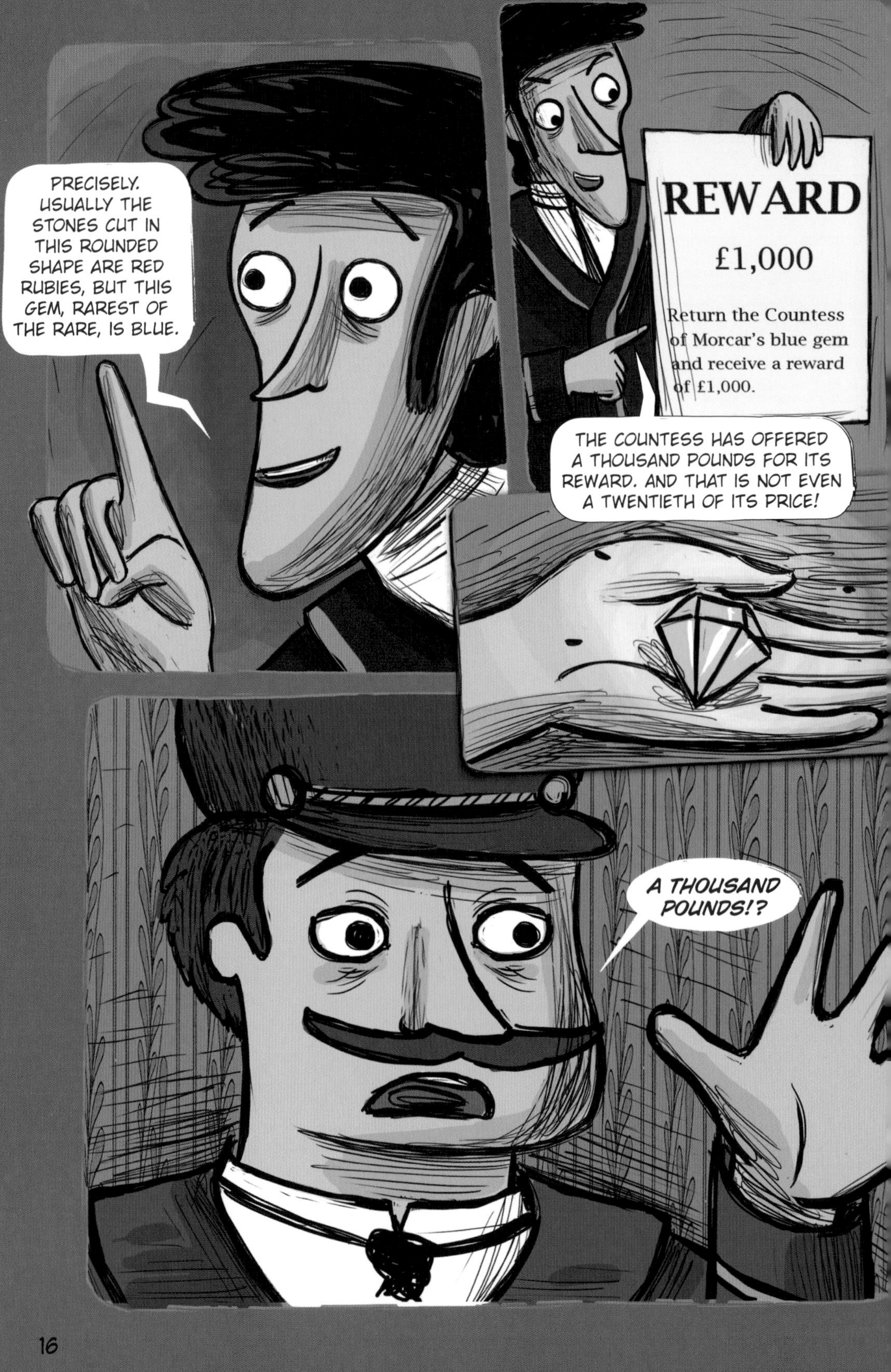
PRECISELY. USUALLY THE STONES CUT IN THIS ROUNDED SHAPE ARE RED RUBIES, BUT THIS GEM, RAREST OF THE RARE, IS BLUE.
REWARD
£1,000
Return the Countess of Morcar's blue gem and receive a reward of £1,000.
THE COUNTESS HAS OFFERED A THOUSAND POUNDS FOR ITS REWARD. AND THAT IS NOT EVEN A TWENTIETH OF ITS PRICE!
A THOUSAND POUNDS!?

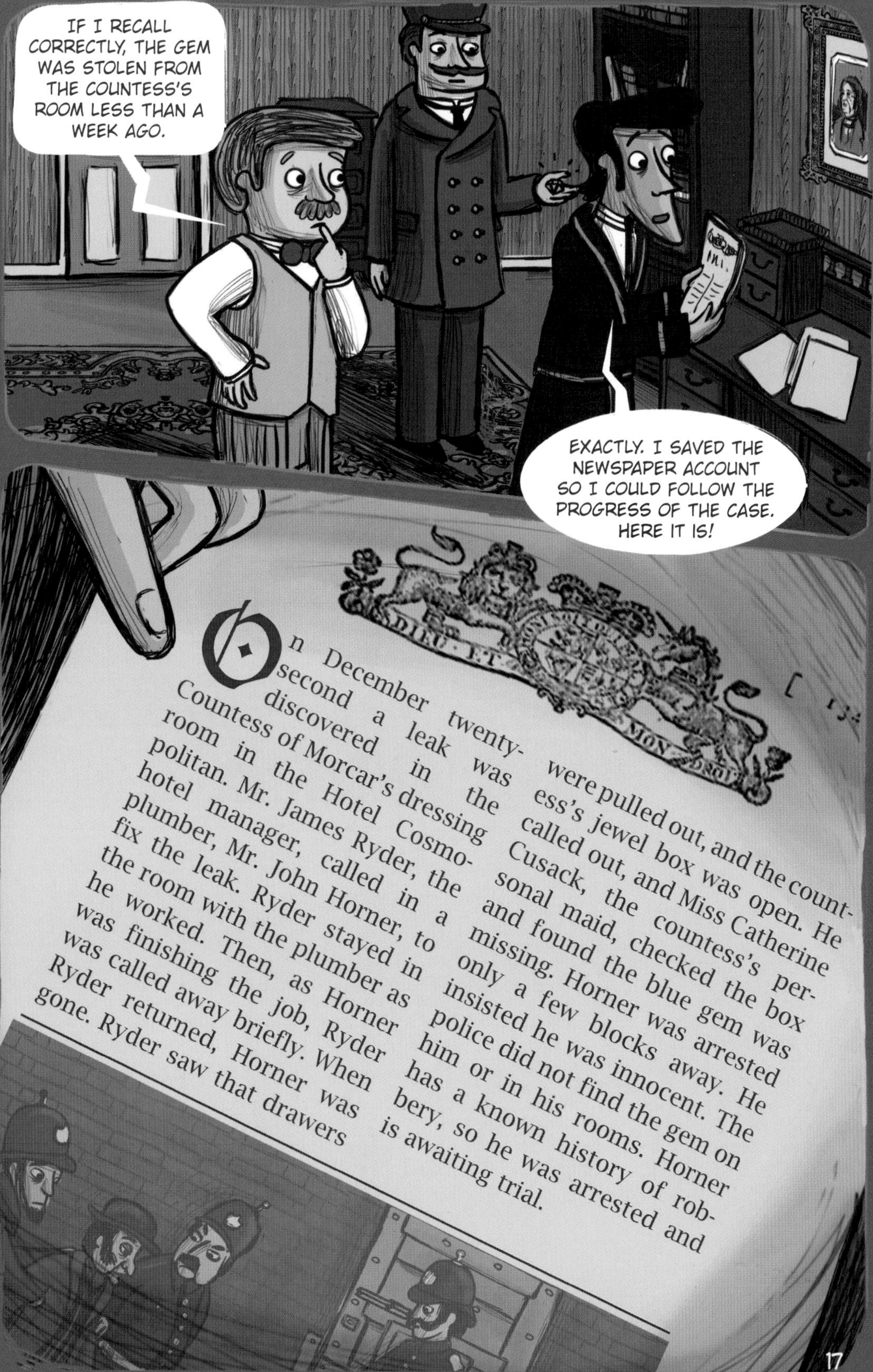
IF I RECALL CORRECTLY, THE GEM WAS STOLEN FROM THE COUNTESS'S ROOM LESS THAN A WEEK AGO.
EXACTLY. I SAVED THE NEWSPAPER ACCOUNT SO I COULD FOLLOW THE PROGRESS OF THE CASE. HERE IT IS!
On December twenty-second a leak was discovered in the Countess of Morcar's dressing room in the Hotel Cosmopolitan. Mr. James Ryder, the hotel manager, called in a plumber, Mr. John Horner, to fix the leak. Ryder stayed in the room with the plumber as he worked. Then, as Horner was finishing the job, Ryder was called away briefly. When Ryder returned, Horner was gone. Ryder saw that drawers
were pulled out, and the countess's jewel box was open. He called out, and Miss Catherine Cusack, the countess's personal maid, checked the box and found the blue gem was missing. Horner was arrested only a few blocks away. He insisted he was innocent. The police did not find the gem on him or in his rooms. Horner has a known history of robbery, so he was arrested and is awaiting trial.

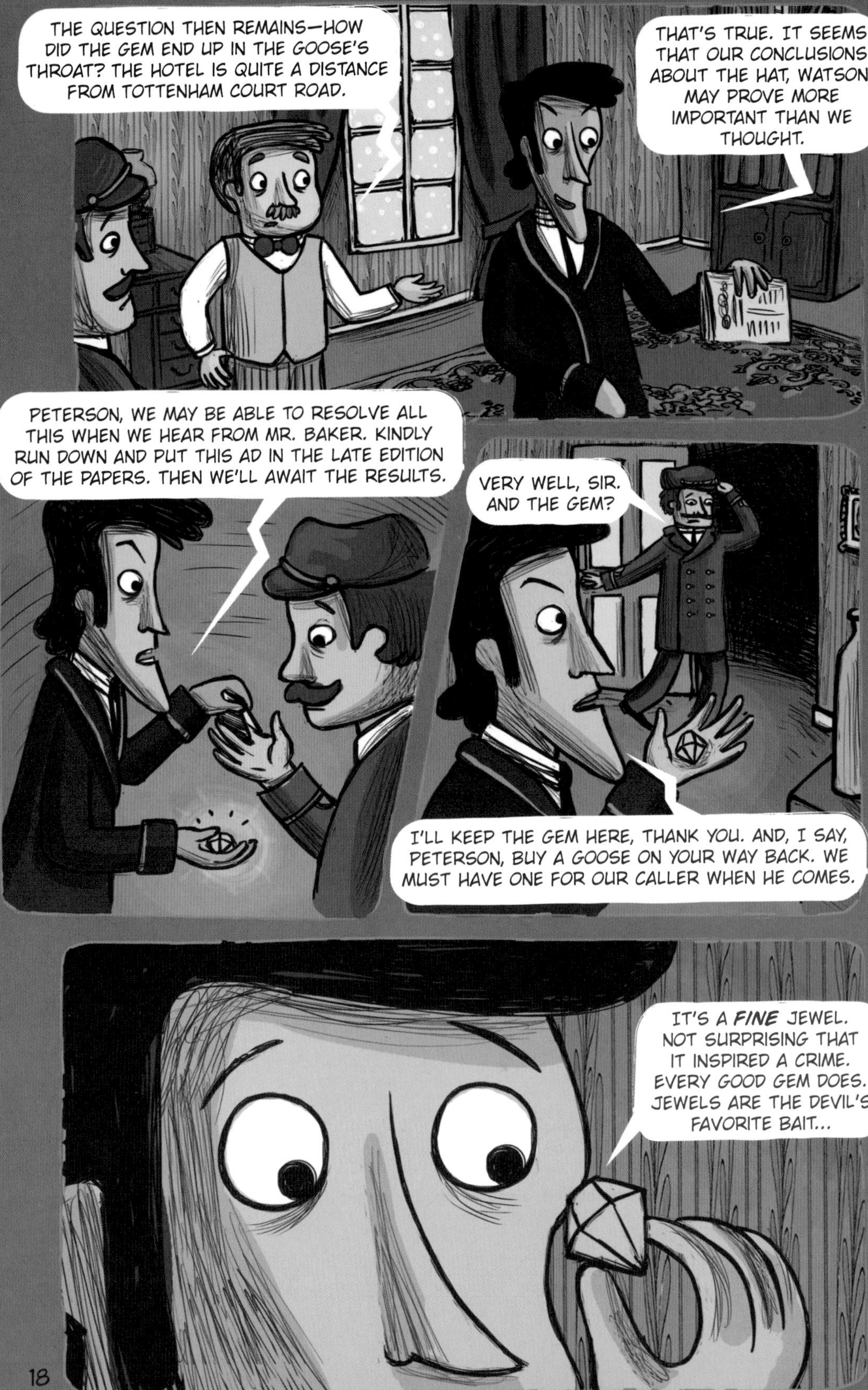
THE QUESTION THEN REMAINS—HOW DID THE GEM END UP IN THE GOOSE'S THROAT? THE HOTEL IS QUITE A DISTANCE FROM TOTTENHAM COURT ROAD.
THAT'S TRUE. IT SEEMS THAT OUR CONCLUSIONS ABOUT THE HAT, WATSON, MAY PROVE MORE IMPORTANT THAN WE THOUGHT.
PETERSON, WE MAY BE ABLE TO RESOLVE ALL THIS WHEN WE HEAR FROM MR. BAKER. KINDLY RUN DOWN AND PUT THIS AD IN THE LATE EDITION OF THE PAPERS. THEN WE'LL AWAIT THE RESULTS.
VERY WELL, SIR. AND THE GEM?
I'LL KEEP THE GEM HERE, THANK YOU. AND, I SAY, PETERSON, BUY A GOOSE ON YOUR WAY BACK. WE MUST HAVE ONE FOR OUR CALLER WHEN HE COMES.
IT'S A ***FINE*** JEWEL. NOT SURPRISING THAT IT INSPIRED A CRIME. EVERY GOOD GEM DOES. JEWELS ARE THE DEVIL'S FAVORITE BAIT...

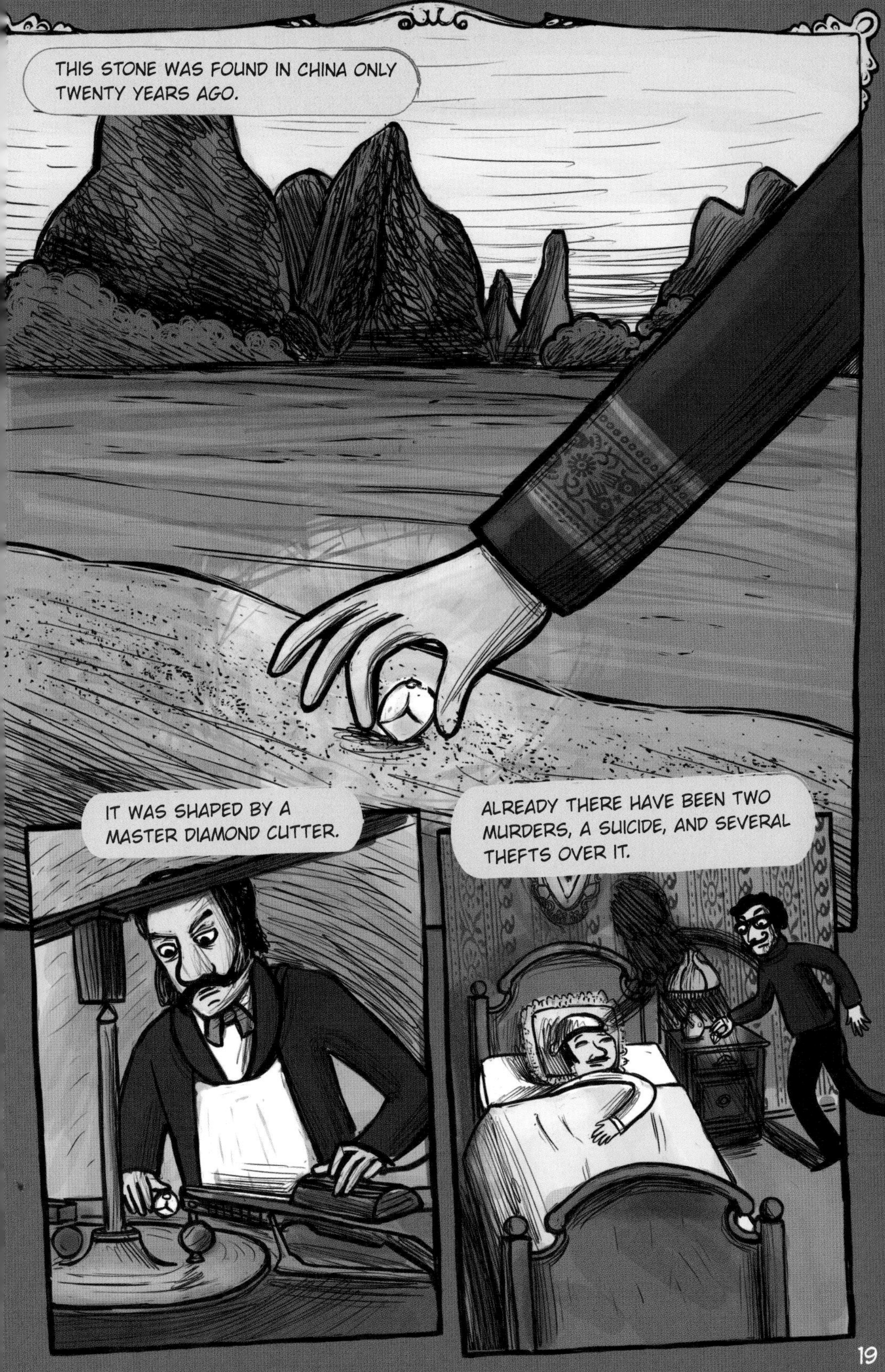
THIS STONE WAS FOUND IN CHINA ONLY TWENTY YEARS AGO.
IT WAS SHAPED BY A MASTER DIAMOND CUTTER.
ALREADY THERE HAVE BEEN TWO MURDERS, A SUICIDE, AND SEVERAL THEFTS OVER IT.

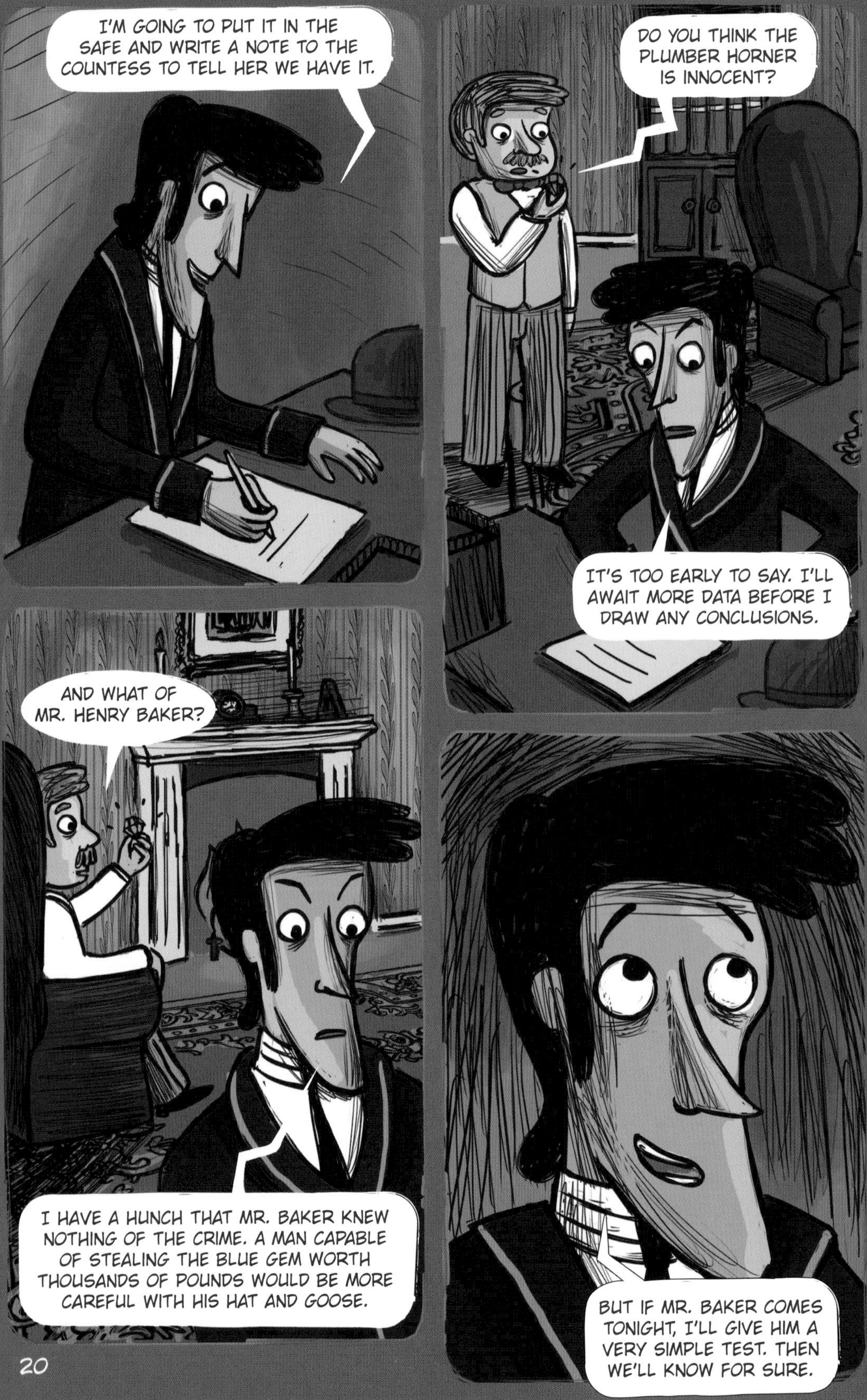
I'M GOING TO PUT IT IN THE SAFE AND WRITE A NOTE TO THE COUNTESS TO TELL HER WE HAVE IT.
DO YOU THINK THE PLUMBER HORNER IS INNOCENT?
IT'S TOO EARLY TO SAY. I'LL AWAIT MORE DATA BEFORE I DRAW ANY CONCLUSIONS.
AND WHAT OF MR. HENRY BAKER?
I HAVE A HUNCH THAT MR. BAKER KNEW NOTHING OF THE CRIME. A MAN CAPABLE OF STEALING THE BLUE GEM WORTH THOUSANDS OF POUNDS WOULD BE MORE CAREFUL WITH HIS HAT AND GOOSE.
BUT IF MR. BAKER COMES TONIGHT, I'LL GIVE HIM A VERY SIMPLE TEST. THEN WE'LL KNOW FOR SURE.

Having finished his note, Holmes pulled out his violin to play one of Beethoven's sonatas, and I made my exit. I had plenty of time to visit patients before the evening's excitement would begin.

At about six-thirty, I returned to Baker Street. I was just taking off my coat when I heard a knock at the door.

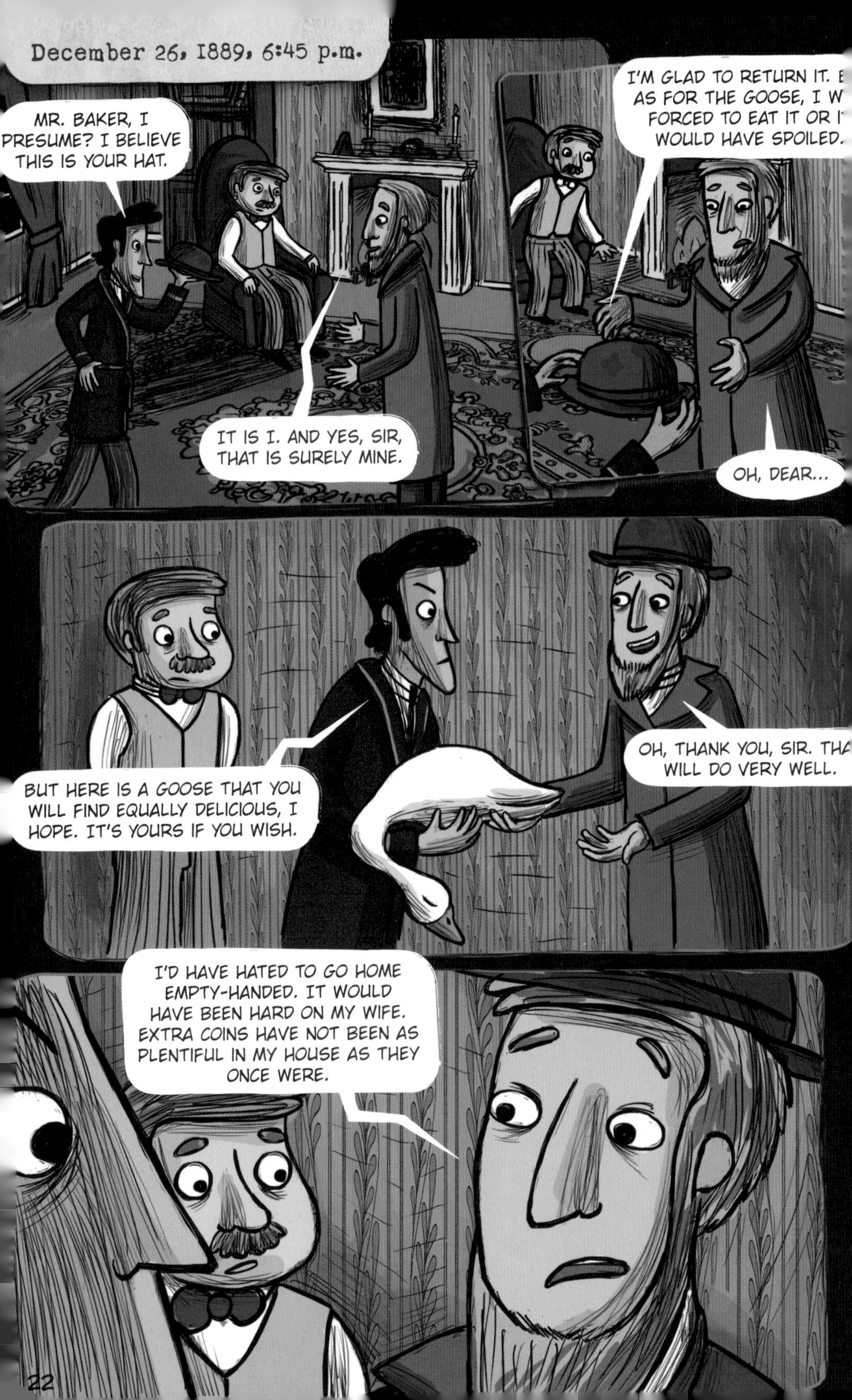
December 26, 1889, 6:45 p.m.
MR. BAKER, I PRESUME? I BELIEVE THIS IS YOUR HAT.
IT IS I. AND YES, SIR, THAT IS SURELY MINE.
I'M GLAD TO RETURN IT. B AS FOR THE GOOSE, I W FORCED TO EAT IT OR I WOULD HAVE SPOILED.
OH, DEAR...
BUT HERE IS A GOOSE THAT YOU WILL FIND EQUALLY DELICIOUS, I HOPE. IT'S YOURS IF YOU WISH.
OH, THANK YOU, SIR. THA WILL DO VERY WELL.
I'D HAVE HATED TO GO HOME EMPTY-HANDED. IT WOULD HAVE BEEN HARD ON MY WIFE. EXTRA COINS HAVE NOT BEEN AS PLENTIFUL IN MY HOUSE AS THEY ONCE WERE.

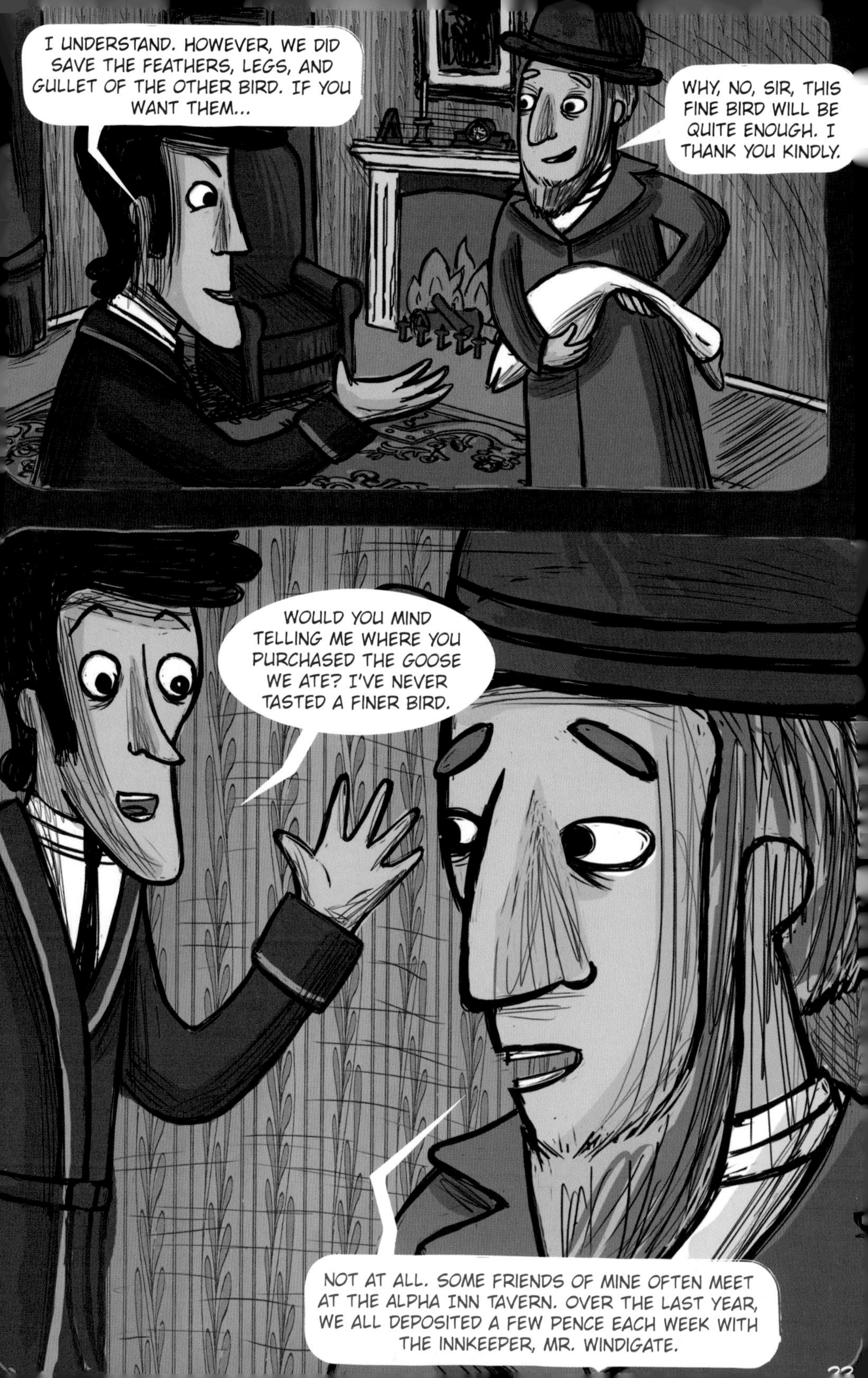
I UNDERSTAND. HOWEVER, WE DID SAVE THE FEATHERS, LEGS, AND GULLET OF THE OTHER BIRD. IF YOU WANT THEM...
WHY, NO, SIR, THIS FINE BIRD WILL BE QUITE ENOUGH. I THANK YOU KINDLY.
WOULD YOU MIND TELLING ME WHERE YOU PURCHASED THE GOOSE WE ATE? I'VE NEVER TASTED A FINER BIRD.
NOT AT ALL. SOME FRIENDS OF MINE OFTEN MEET AT THE ALPHA INN TAVERN. OVER THE LAST YEAR, WE ALL DEPOSITED A FEW PENCE EACH WEEK WITH THE INNKEEPER, MR. WINDIGATE.

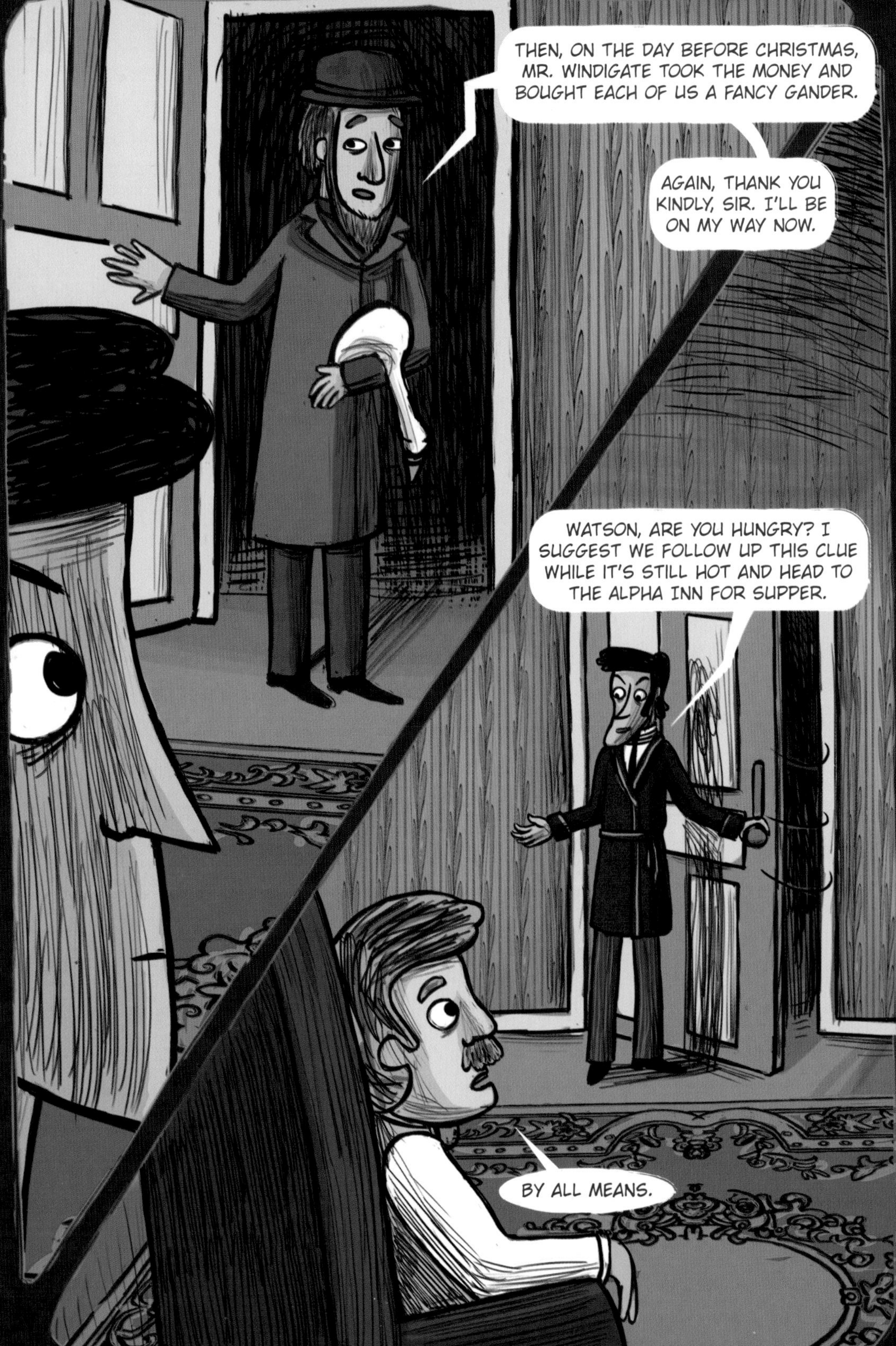
THEN, ON THE DAY BEFORE CHRISTMAS, MR. WINDIGATE TOOK THE MONEY AND BOUGHT EACH OF US A FANCY GANDER.
AGAIN, THANK YOU KINDLY, SIR. I'LL BE ON MY WAY NOW.
WATSON, ARE YOU HUNGRY? I SUGGEST WE FOLLOW UP THIS CLUE WHILE IT'S STILL HOT AND HEAD TO THE ALPHA INN FOR SUPPER.
BY ALL MEANS.

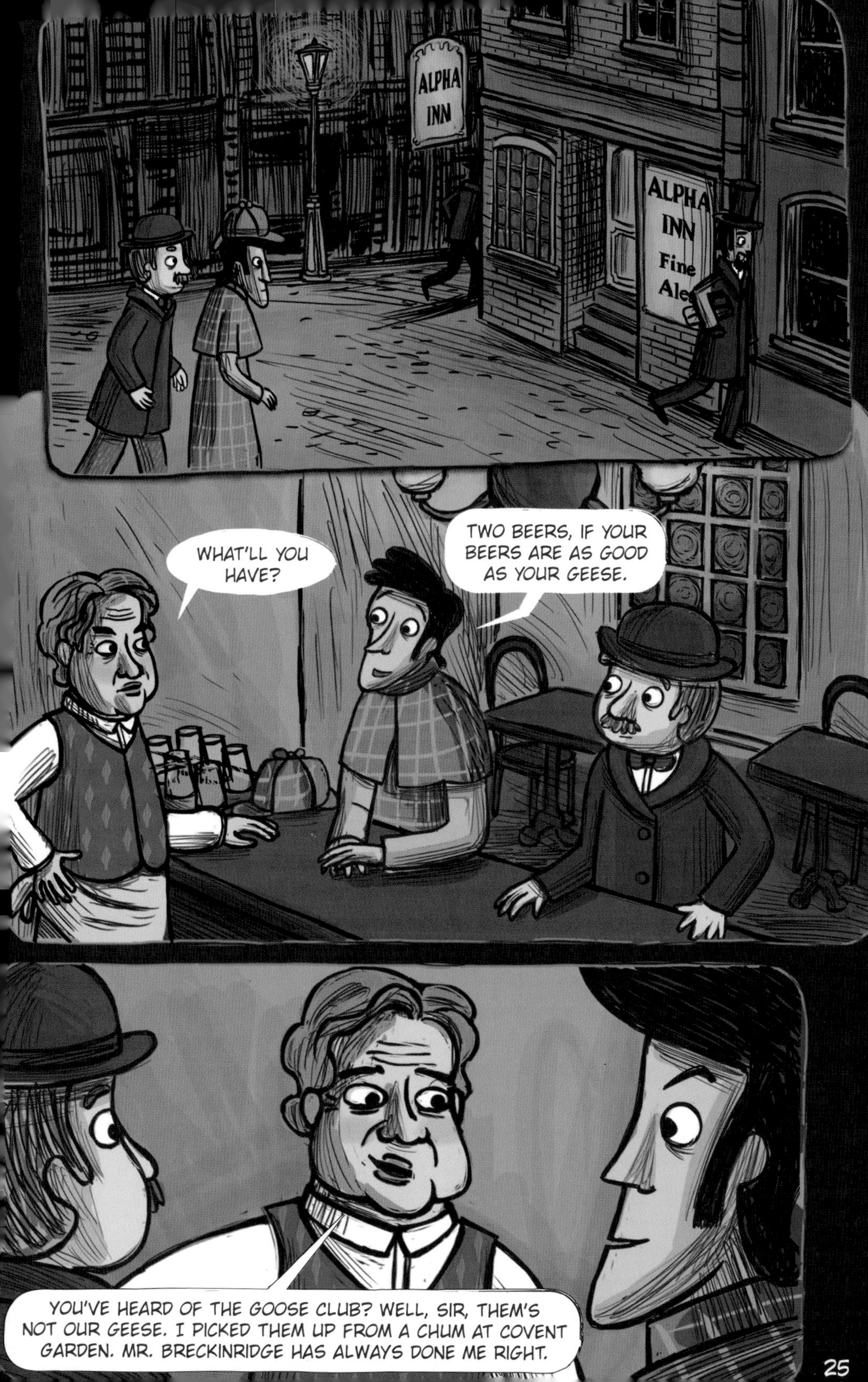
ALPHA INN
ALPHA INN Fine Ale
WHAT'LL YOU HAVE?
TWO BEERS, IF YOUR BEERS ARE AS GOOD AS YOUR GEESE.
YOU'VE HEARD OF THE GOOSE CLUB? WELL, SIR, THEM'S NOT OUR GEESE. I PICKED THEM UP FROM A CHUM AT COVENT GARDEN. MR. BRECKINRIDGE HAS ALWAYS DONE ME RIGHT.

After downing our beers along with a fine pub meal, we tipped our host and headed for the Covent Garden Market. We arrived just as Breckinridge was closing his stall for the evening.

ALPHA INN
ALPHA INN
Fine Ale

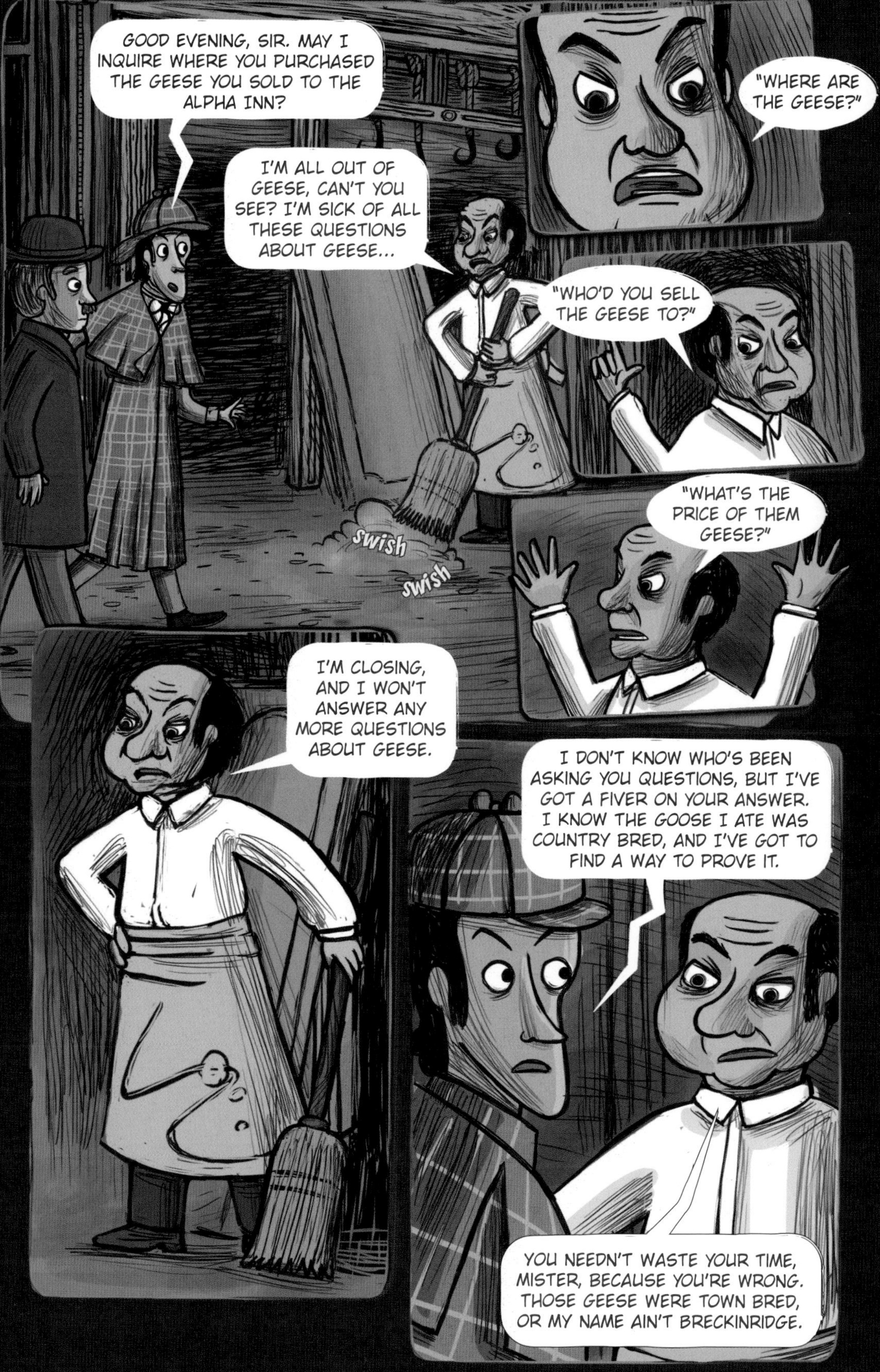
GOOD EVENING, SIR. MAY I INQUIRE WHERE YOU PURCHASED THE GEESE YOU SOLD TO THE ALPHA INN?
I'M ALL OUT OF GEESE, CAN'T YOU SEE? I'M SICK OF ALL THESE QUESTIONS ABOUT GEESE...
SWISH
SWISH
"WHERE ARE THE GEESE?"
"WHO'D YOU SELL THE GEESE TO?"
"WHAT'S THE PRICE OF THEM GEESE?"
I'M CLOSING, AND I WON'T ANSWER ANY MORE QUESTIONS ABOUT GEESE.
I DON'T KNOW WHO'S BEEN ASKING YOU QUESTIONS, BUT I'VE GOT A FIVER ON YOUR ANSWER. I KNOW THE GOOSE I ATE WAS COUNTRY BRED, AND I'VE GOT TO FIND A WAY TO PROVE IT.
YOU NEEDN'T WASTE YOUR TIME, MISTER, BECAUSE YOU'RE WRONG. THOSE GEESE WERE TOWN BRED, OR MY NAME AIN'T BRECKINRIDGE.

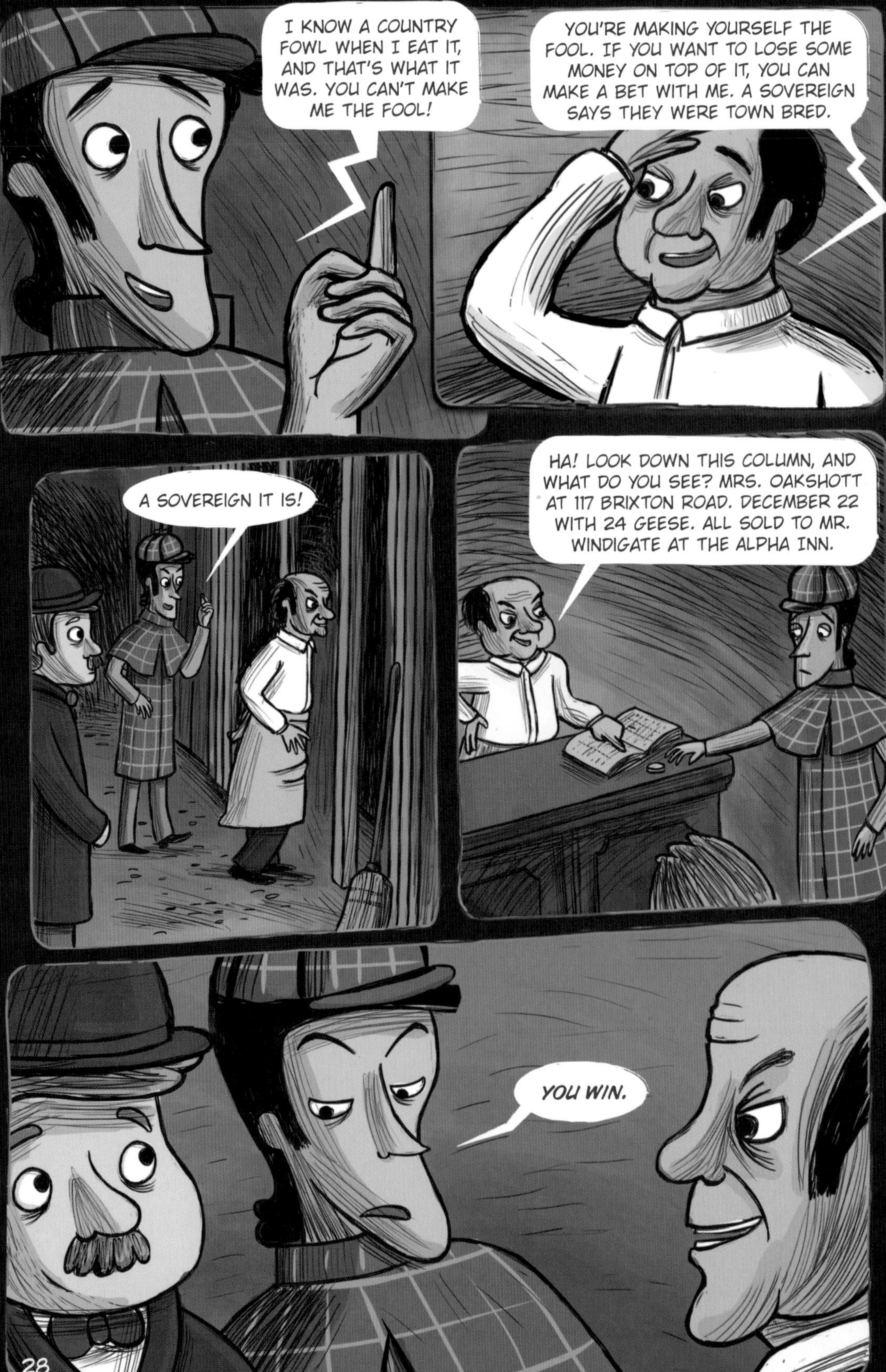

I KNOW A COUNTRY FOWL WHEN I EAT IT, AND THAT'S WHAT IT WAS. YOU CAN'T MAKE ME THE FOOL!
YOU'RE MAKING YOURSELF THE FOOL. IF YOU WANT TO LOSE SOME MONEY ON TOP OF IT, YOU CAN MAKE A BET WITH ME. A SOVEREIGN SAYS THEY WERE TOWN BRED.
A SOVEREIGN IT IS!
HA! LOOK DOWN THIS COLUMN, AND WHAT DO YOU SEE? MRS. OAKSHOTT AT 117 BRIXTON ROAD. DECEMBER 22 WITH 24 GEESE. ALL SOLD TO MR. WINDIGATE AT THE ALPHA INN.
YOU WIN.

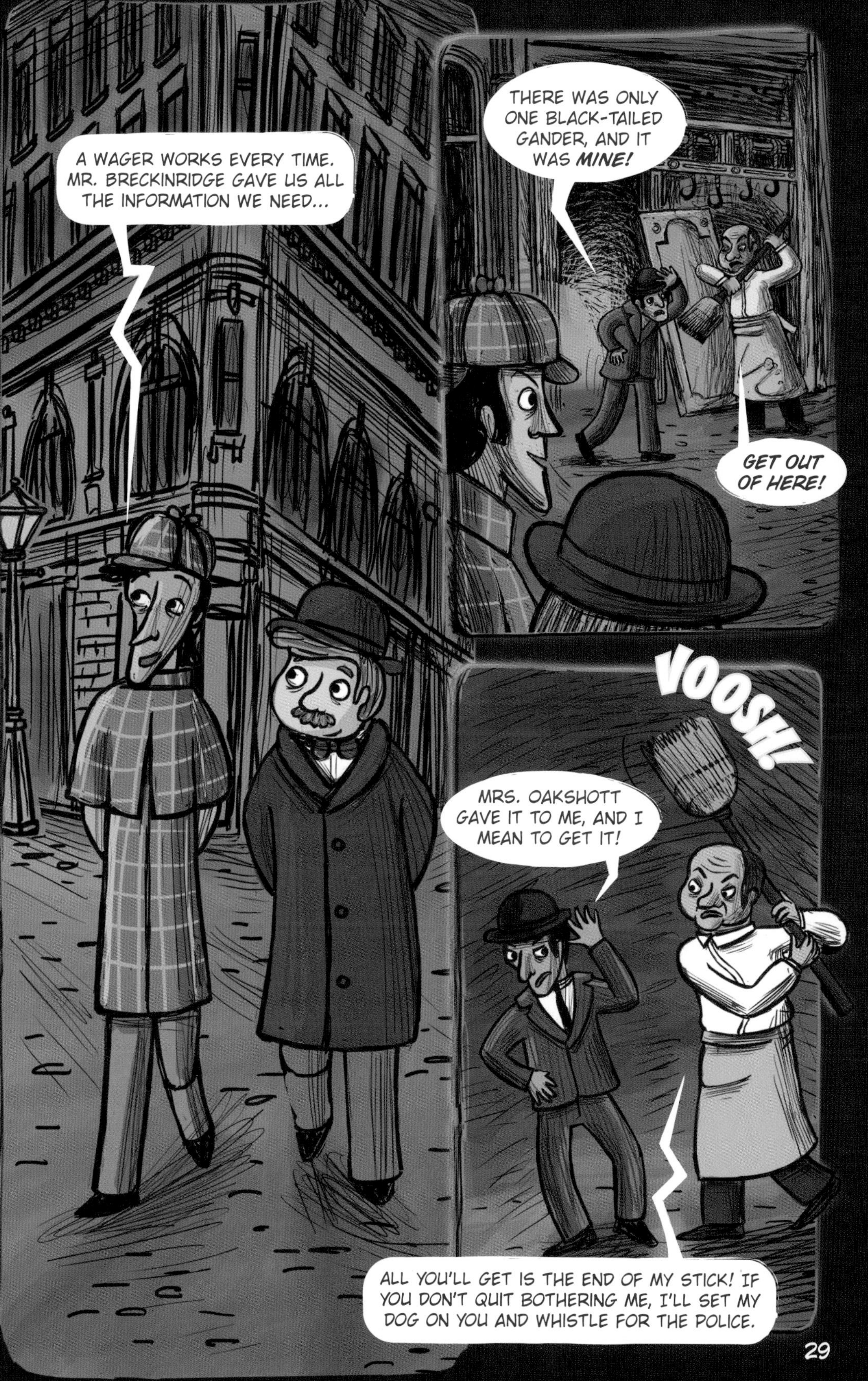
A WAGER WORKS EVERY TIME. MR. BRECKINRIDGE GAVE US ALL THE INFORMATION WE NEED...
THERE WAS ONLY ONE BLACK-TAILED GANDER, AND IT WAS *MINE!*
GET OUT OF HERE!
VOOSH!
MRS. OAKSHOTT GAVE IT TO ME, AND I MEAN TO GET IT!
ALL YOU'LL GET IS THE END OF MY STICK! IF YOU DON'T QUIT BOTHERING ME, I'LL SET MY DOG ON YOU AND WHISTLE FOR THE POLICE.

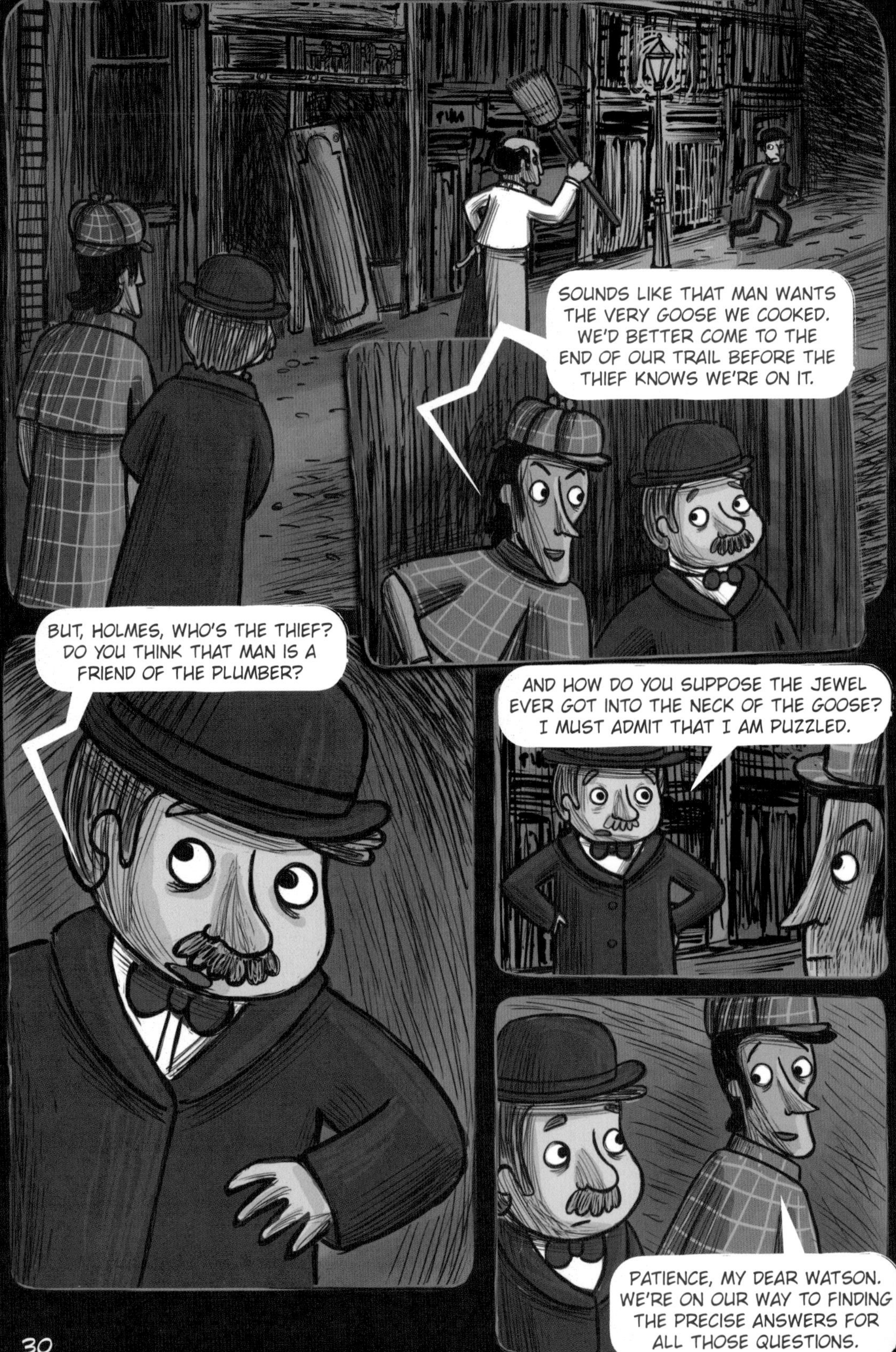
SOUNDS LIKE THAT MAN WANTS THE VERY GOOSE WE COOKED. WE'D BETTER COME TO THE END OF OUR TRAIL BEFORE THE THIEF KNOWS WE'RE ON IT.
BUT, HOLMES, WHO'S THE THIEF? DO YOU THINK THAT MAN IS A FRIEND OF THE PLUMBER?
AND HOW DO YOU SUPPOSE THE JEWEL EVER GOT INTO THE NECK OF THE GOOSE? I MUST ADMIT THAT I AM PUZZLED.
PATIENCE, MY DEAR WATSON. WE'RE ON OUR WAY TO FINDING THE PRECISE ANSWERS FOR ALL THOSE QUESTIONS.

My mind was still muddled, but Holmes had a plan. We hailed a cab to Brixton Road and came to Mrs. Oakshott's farm. We knocked at the door of the small stone house, and a young woman answered.

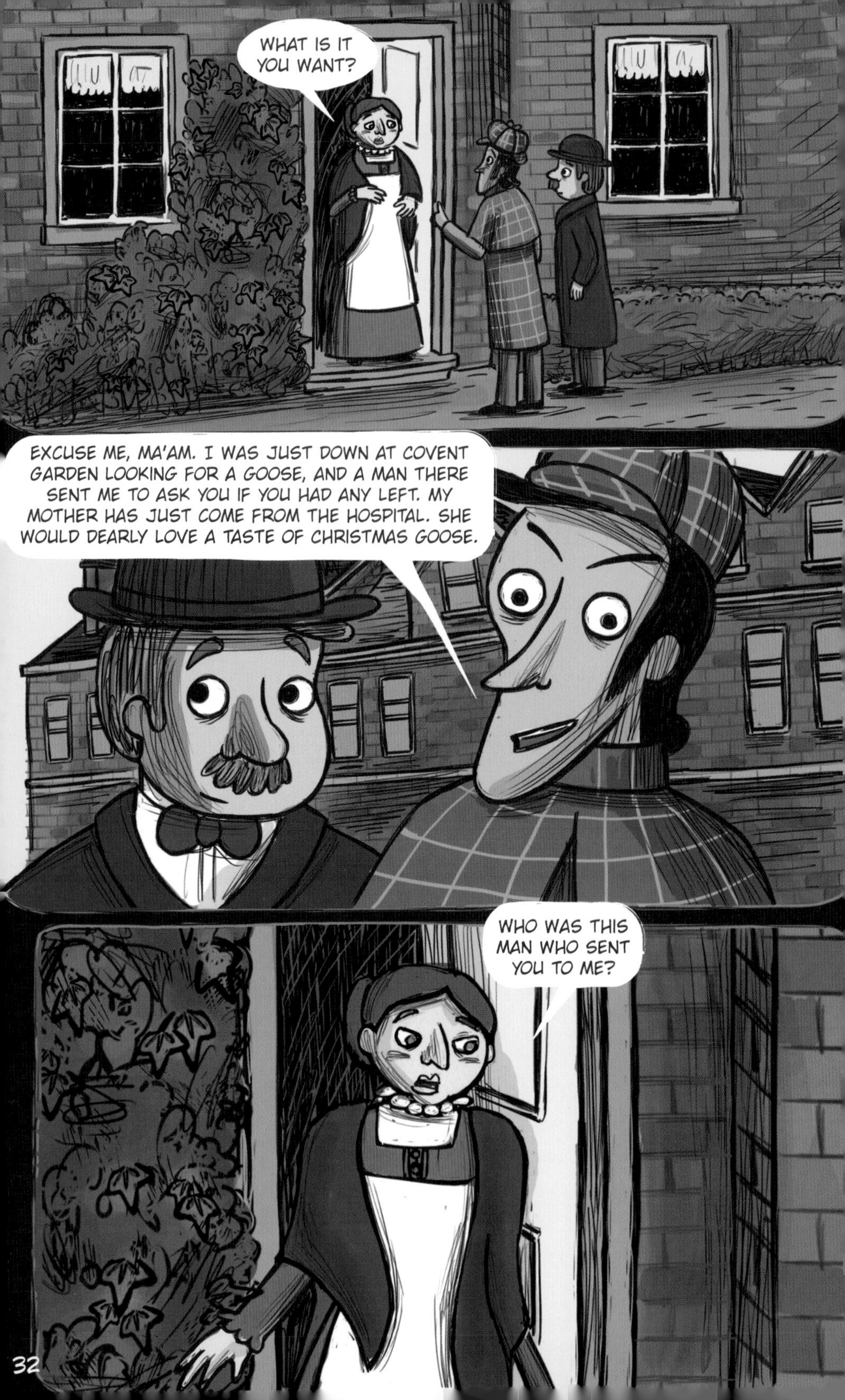
WHAT IS IT YOU WANT?
EXCUSE ME, MA'AM. I WAS JUST DOWN AT COVENT GARDEN LOOKING FOR A GOOSE, AND A MAN THERE SENT ME TO ASK YOU IF YOU HAD ANY LEFT. MY MOTHER HAS JUST COME FROM THE HOSPITAL. SHE WOULD DEARLY LOVE A TASTE OF CHRISTMAS GOOSE.
WHO WAS THIS MAN WHO SENT YOU TO ME?

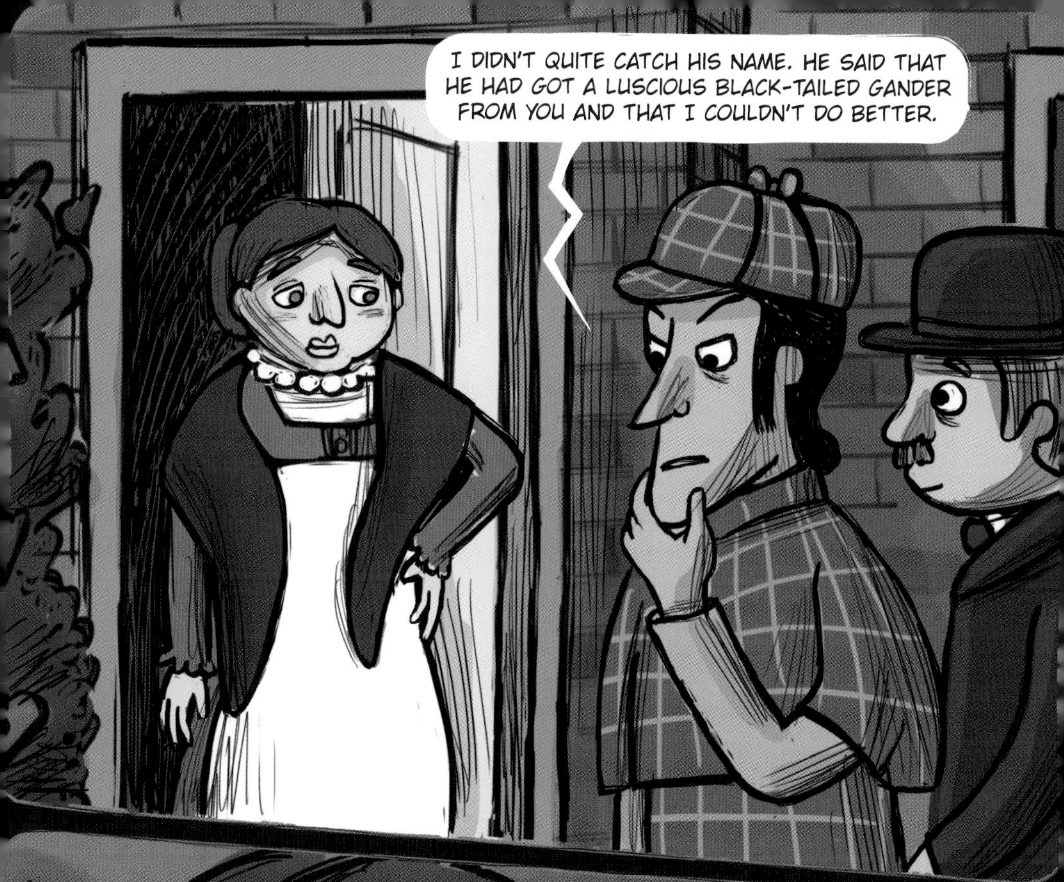
I DIDN'T QUITE CATCH HIS NAME. HE SAID THAT HE HAD GOT A LUSCIOUS BLACK-TAILED GANDER FROM YOU AND THAT I COULDN'T DO BETTER.

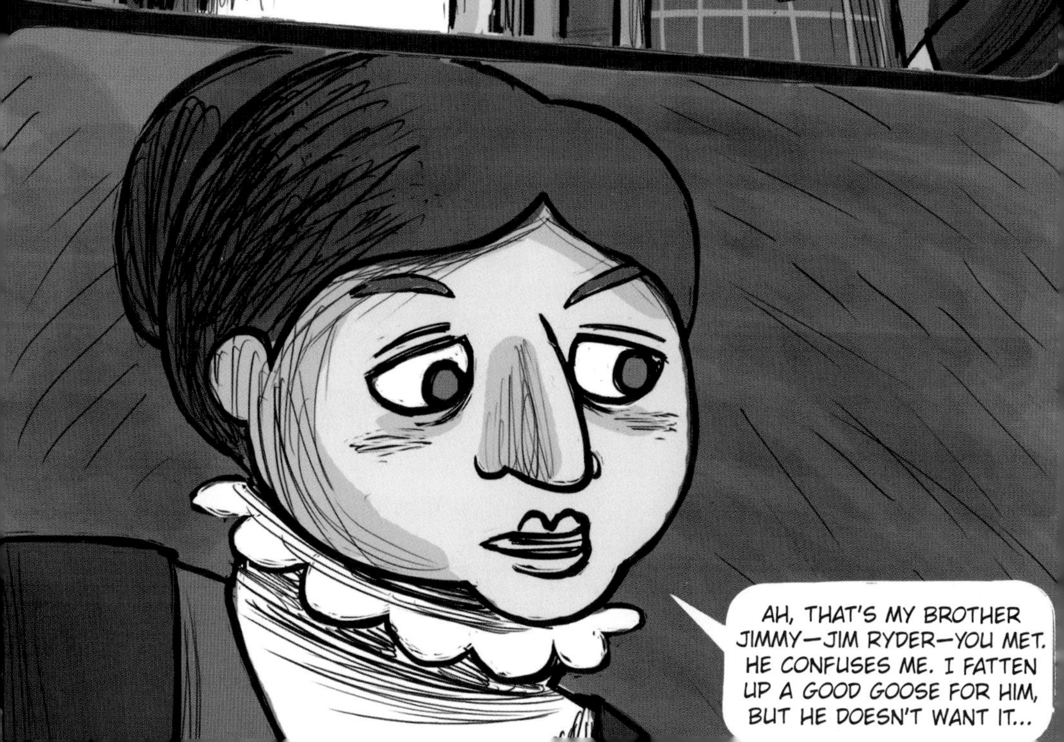
AH, THAT'S MY BROTHER JIMMY—JIM RYDER—YOU MET. HE CONFUSES ME. I FATTEN UP A GOOD GOOSE FOR HIM, BUT HE DOESN'T WANT IT...

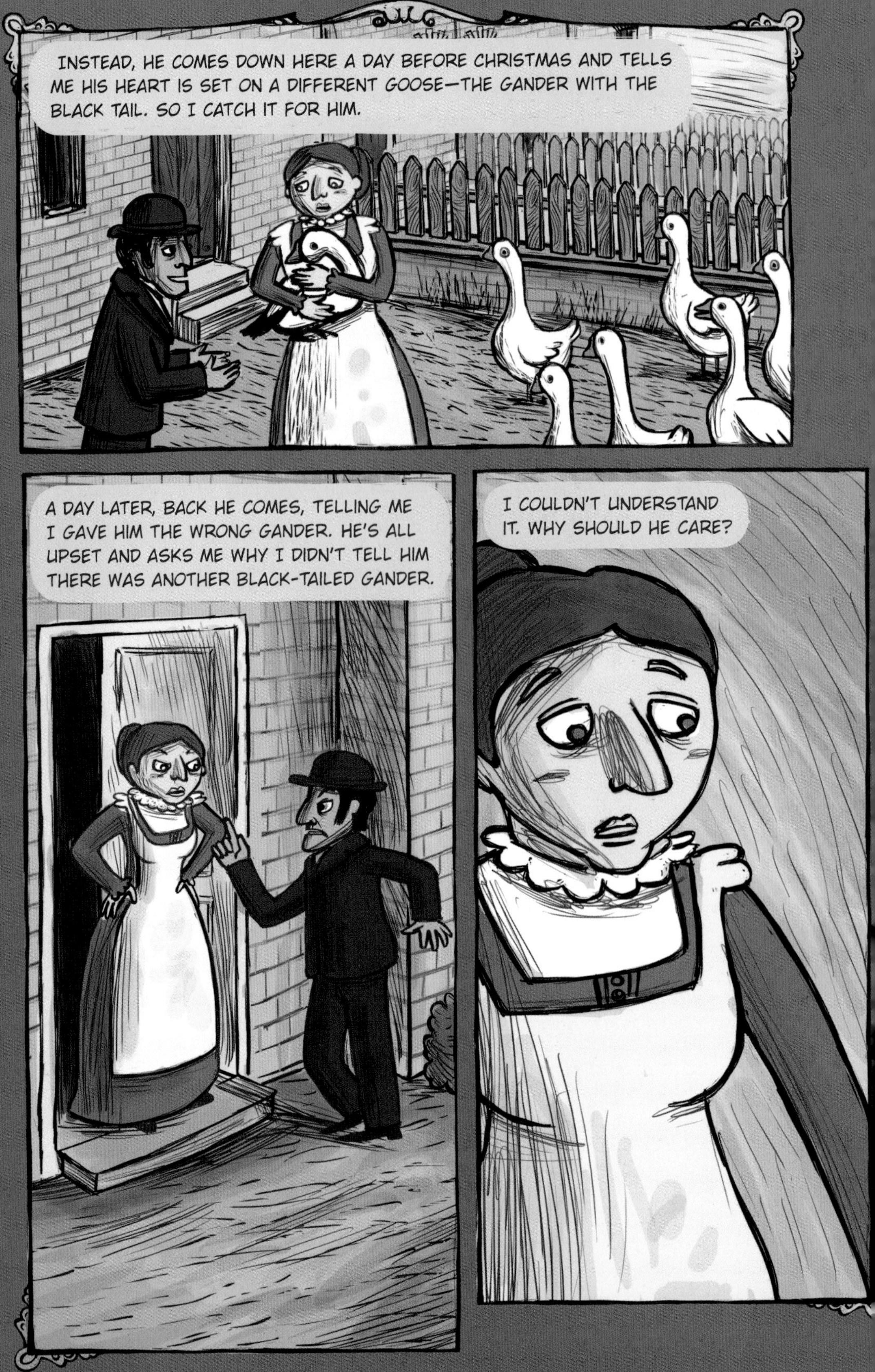
INSTEAD, HE COMES DOWN HERE A DAY BEFORE CHRISTMAS AND TELLS ME HIS HEART IS SET ON A DIFFERENT GOOSE—THE GANDER WITH THE BLACK TAIL. SO I CATCH IT FOR HIM.
A DAY LATER, BACK HE COMES, TELLING ME I GAVE HIM THE WRONG GANDER. HE'S ALL UPSET AND ASKS ME WHY I DIDN'T TELL HIM THERE WAS ANOTHER BLACK-TAILED GANDER.
I COULDN'T UNDERSTAND IT. WHY SHOULD HE CARE?

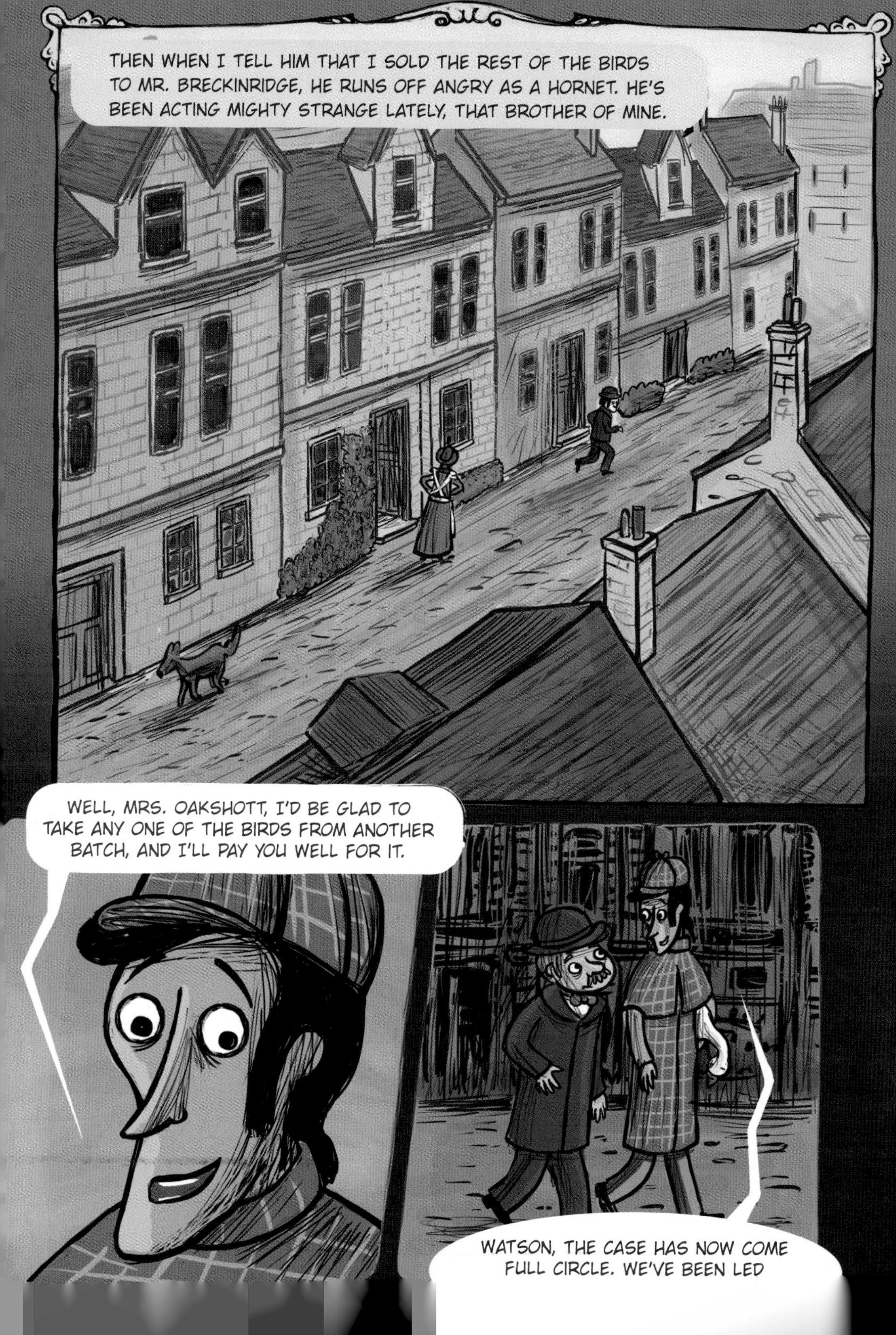
THEN WHEN I TELL HIM THAT I SOLD THE REST OF THE BIRDS TO MR. BRECKINRIDGE, HE RUNS OFF ANGRY AS A HORNET. HE'S BEEN ACTING MIGHTY STRANGE LATELY, THAT BROTHER OF MINE.
WELL, MRS. OAKSHOTT, I'D BE GLAD TO TAKE ANY ONE OF THE BIRDS FROM ANOTHER BATCH, AND I'LL PAY YOU WELL FOR IT.
WATSON, THE CASE HAS NOW COME FULL CIRCLE. WE'VE BEEN LED

At ten o'clock the next morning, Sherlock Holmes and I took a cab to the Hotel Cosmopolitan. We had an appointment to talk with the manager, James Ryder. When we arrived, we were led into a small study to wait for him. A slender gentleman with sloped shoulders and a thin, snoutlike nose soon entered. I saw immediately that he was the man who had been at Breckinridge's stall.

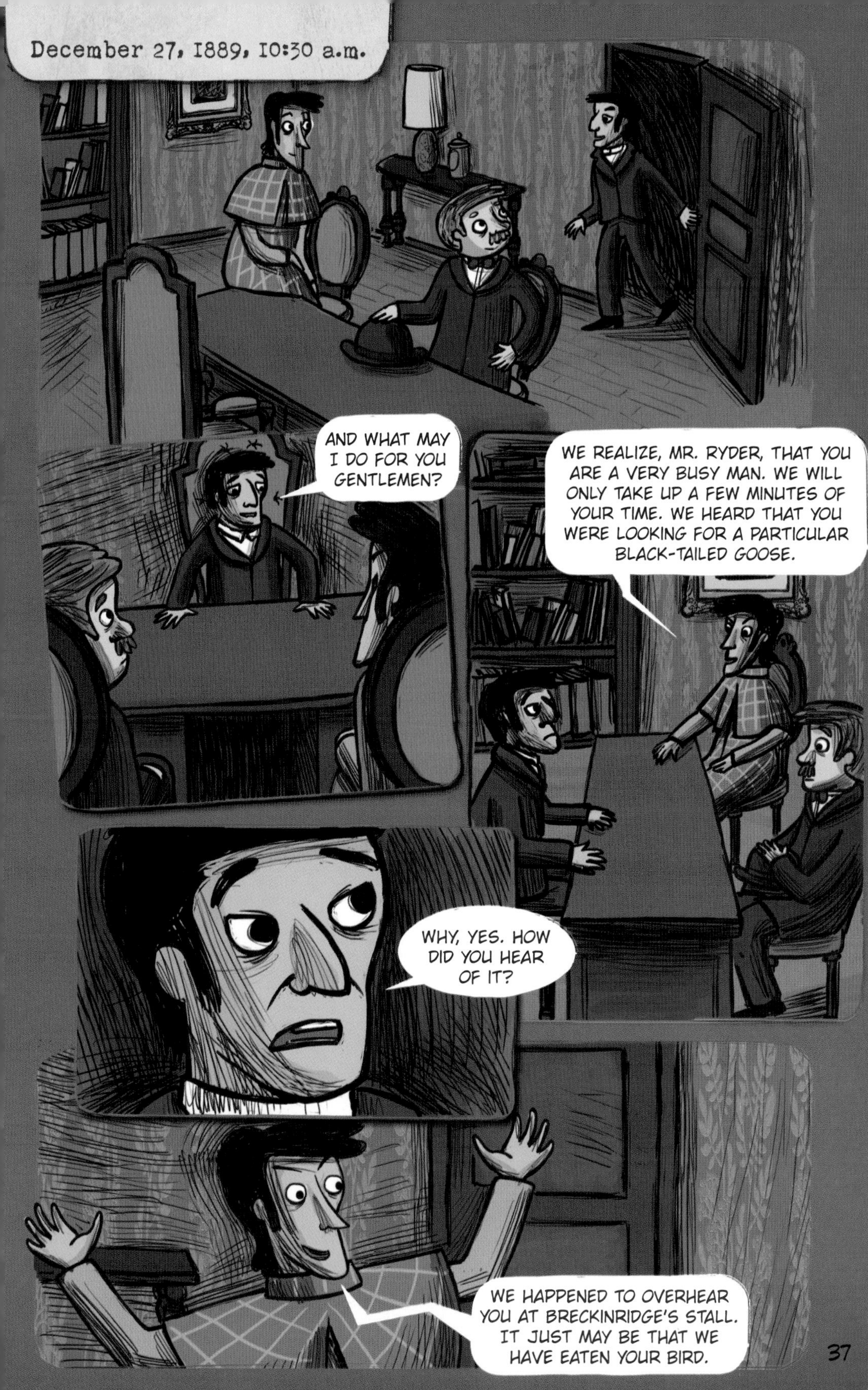
December 27, 1889, 10:30 a.m.
AND WHAT MAY I DO FOR YOU GENTLEMEN?
WE REALIZE, MR. RYDER, THAT YOU ARE A VERY BUSY MAN. WE WILL ONLY TAKE UP A FEW MINUTES OF YOUR TIME. WE HEARD THAT YOU WERE LOOKING FOR A PARTICULAR BLACK-TAILED GOOSE.
WHY, YES. HOW DID YOU HEAR OF IT?
WE HAPPENED TO OVERHEAR YOU AT BRECKINRIDGE'S STALL. IT JUST MAY BE THAT WE HAVE EATEN YOUR BIRD.

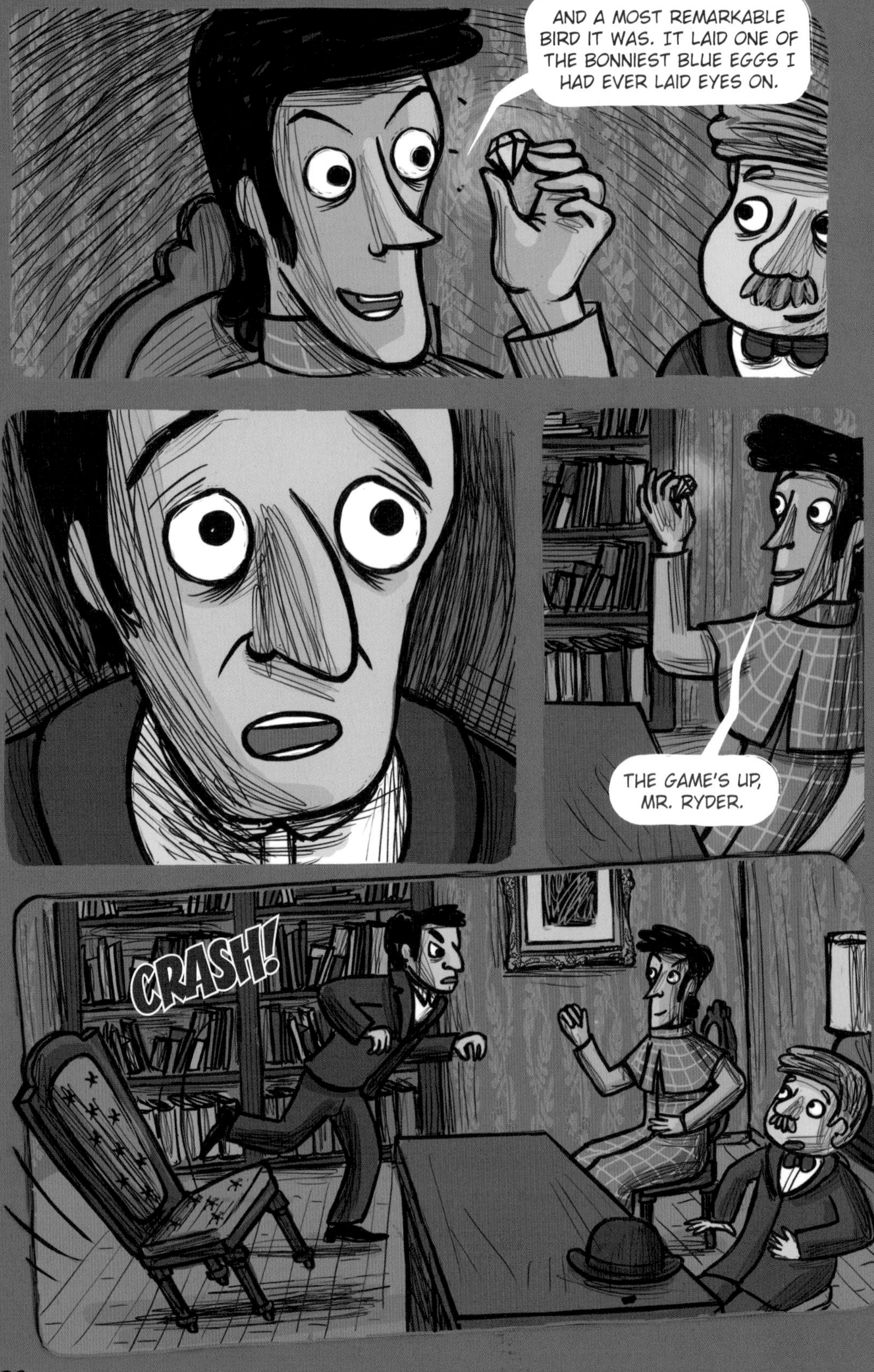
AND A MOST REMARKABLE BIRD IT WAS. IT LAID ONE OF THE BONNIEST BLUE EGGS I HAD EVER LAID EYES ON.
THE GAME'S UP, MR. RYDER.
CRASH!

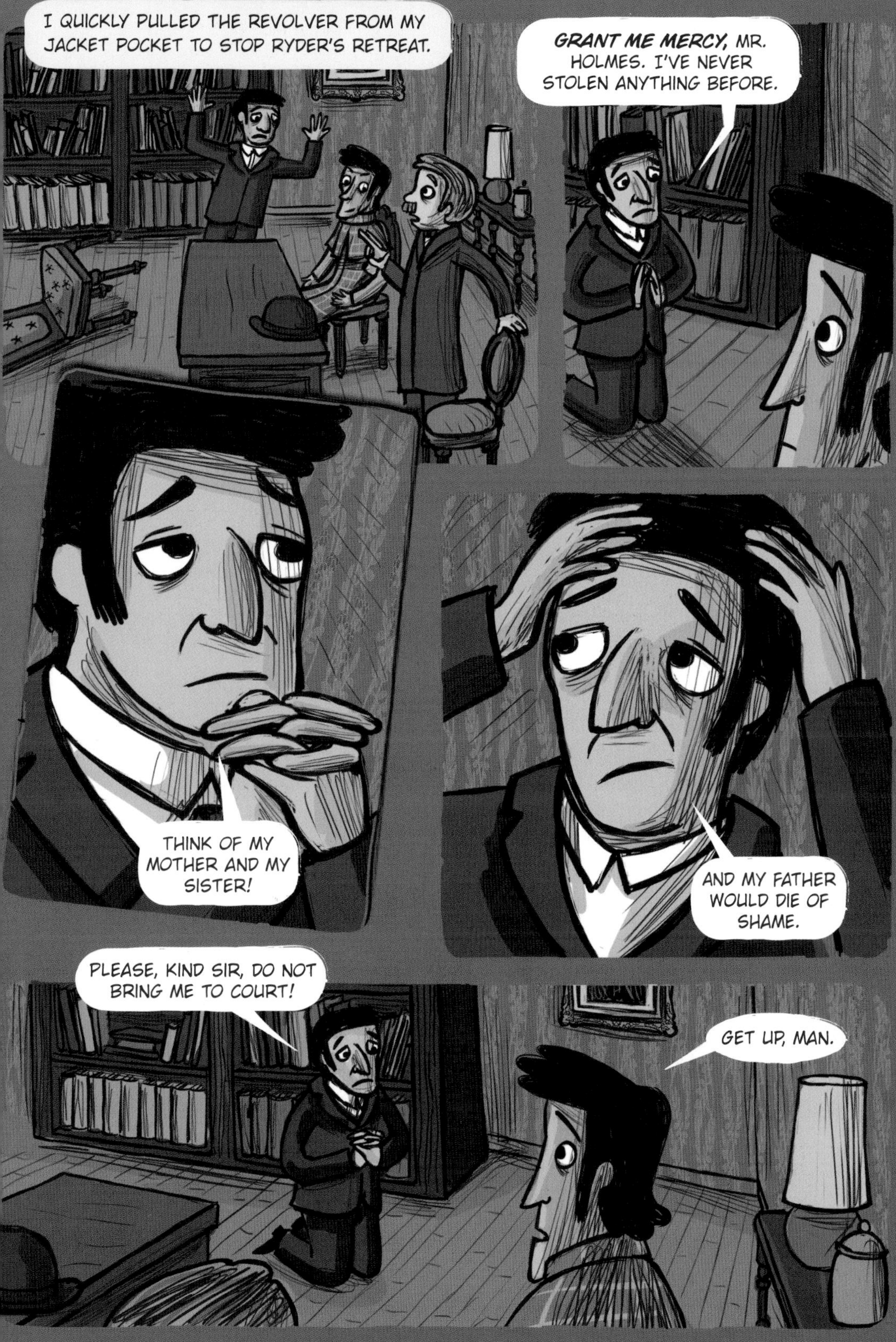
I QUICKLY PULLED THE REVOLVER FROM MY JACKET POCKET TO STOP RYDER'S RETREAT.
GRANT ME MERCY, MR. HOLMES. I'VE NEVER STOLEN ANYTHING BEFORE.
THINK OF MY MOTHER AND MY SISTER!
AND MY FATHER WOULD DIE OF SHAME.
PLEASE, KIND SIR, DO NOT BRING ME TO COURT!
GET UP, MAN.

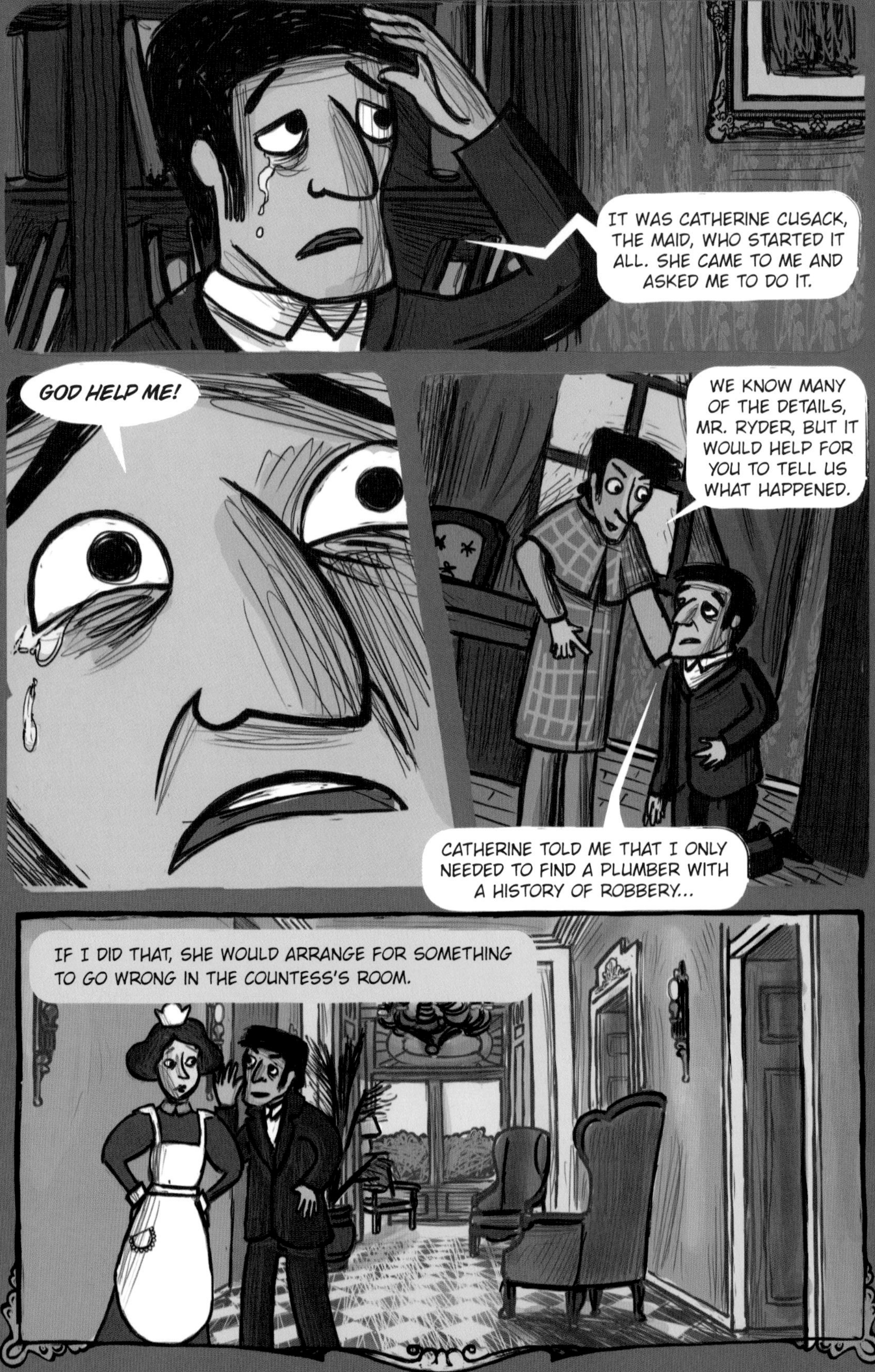
IT WAS CATHERINE CUSACK, THE MAID, WHO STARTED IT ALL. SHE CAME TO ME AND ASKED ME TO DO IT.
GOD HELP ME!
WE KNOW MANY OF THE DETAILS, MR. RYDER, BUT IT WOULD HELP FOR YOU TO TELL US WHAT HAPPENED.
CATHERINE TOLD ME THAT I ONLY NEEDED TO FIND A PLUMBER WITH A HISTORY OF ROBBERY...
IF I DID THAT, SHE WOULD ARRANGE FOR SOMETHING TO GO WRONG IN THE COUNTESS'S ROOM.

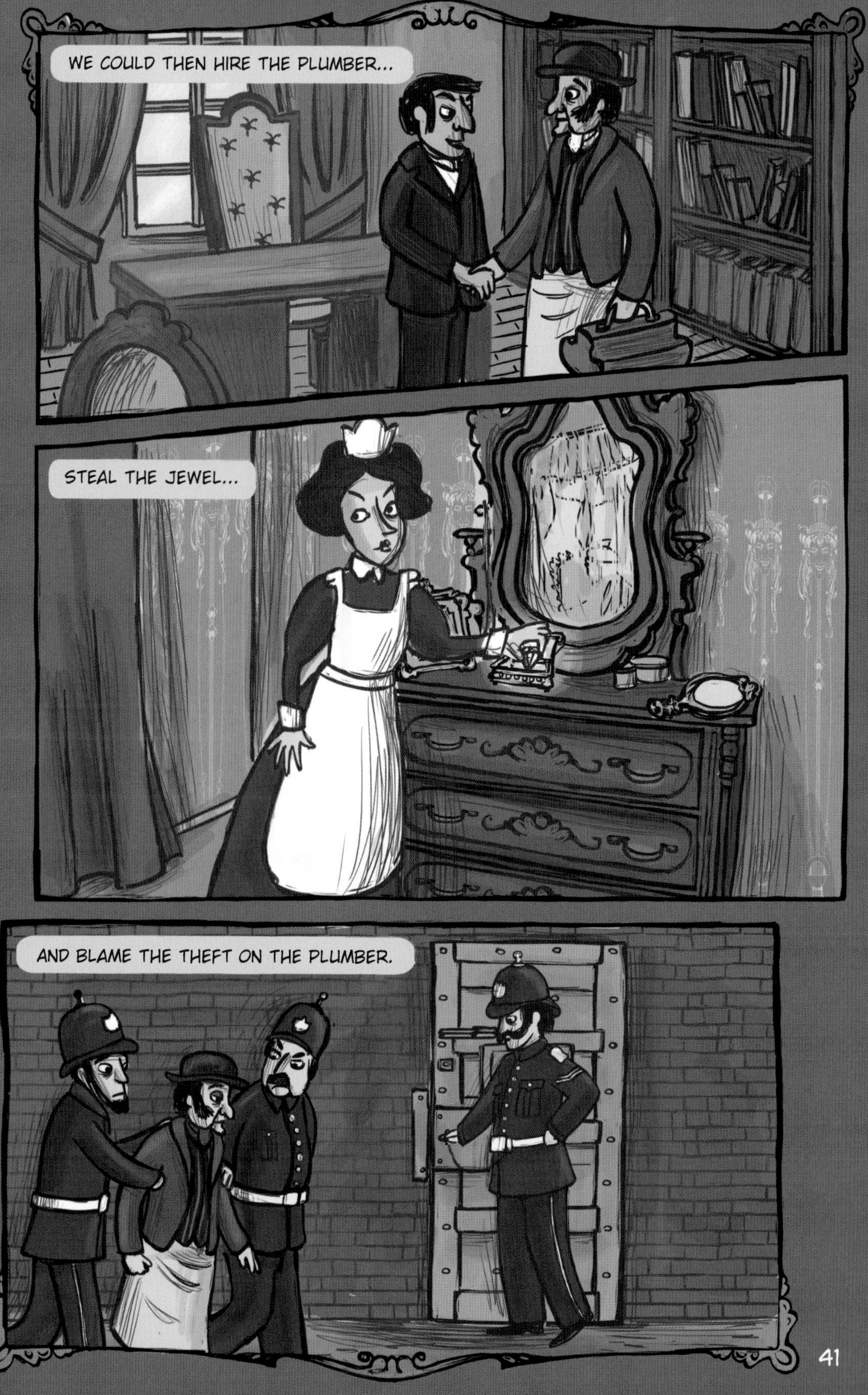
WE COULD THEN HIRE THE PLUMBER...
STEAL THE JEWEL...
AND BLAME THE THEFT ON THE PLUMBER.

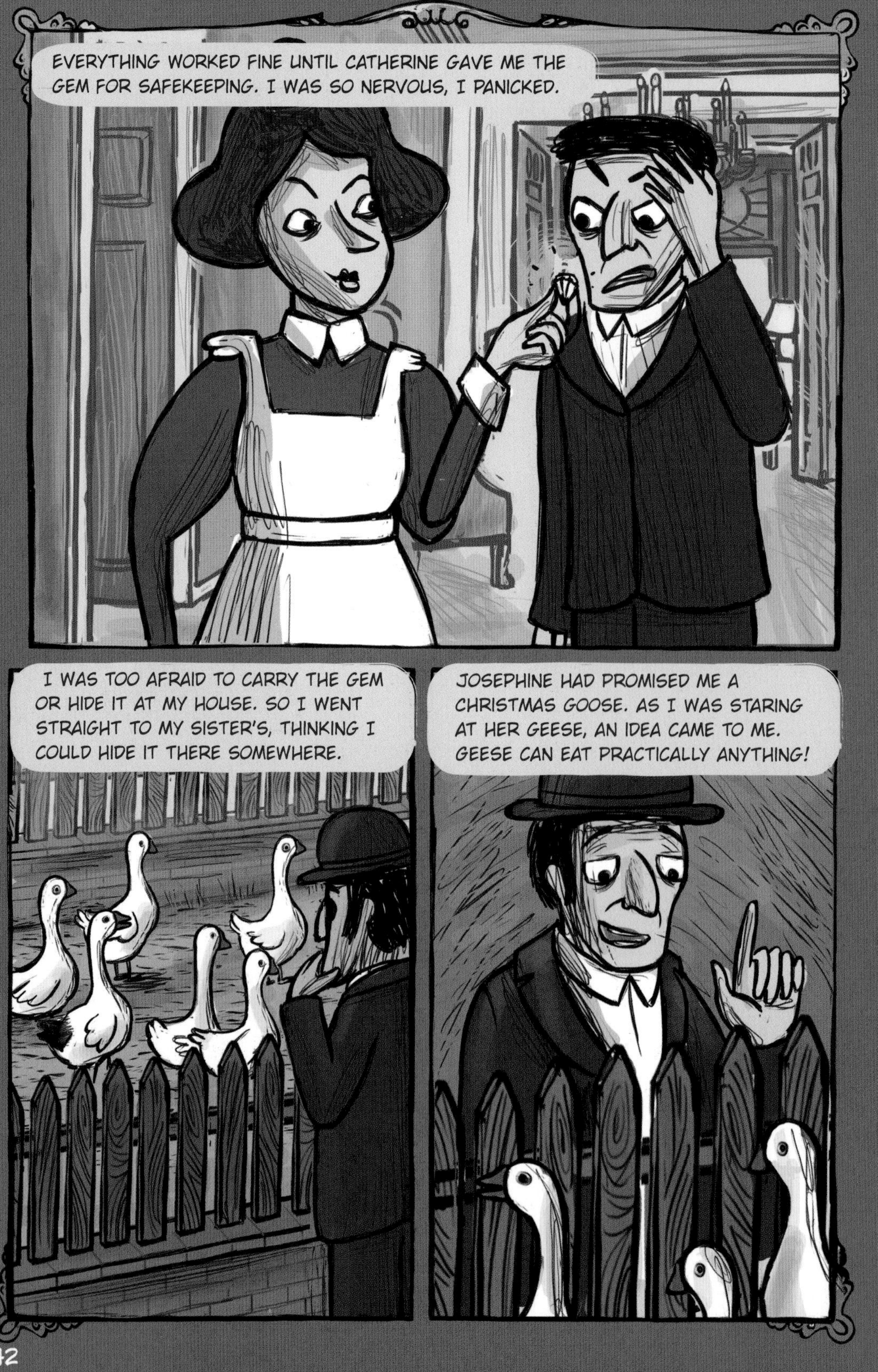
EVERYTHING WORKED FINE UNTIL CATHERINE GAVE ME THE GEM FOR SAFEKEEPING. I WAS SO NERVOUS, I PANICKED.
I WAS TOO AFRAID TO CARRY THE GEM OR HIDE IT AT MY HOUSE. SO I WENT STRAIGHT TO MY SISTER'S, THINKING I COULD HIDE IT THERE SOMEWHERE.
JOSEPHINE HAD PROMISED ME A CHRISTMAS GOOSE. AS I WAS STARING AT HER GEESE, AN IDEA CAME TO ME. GEESE CAN EAT PRACTICALLY ANYTHING!

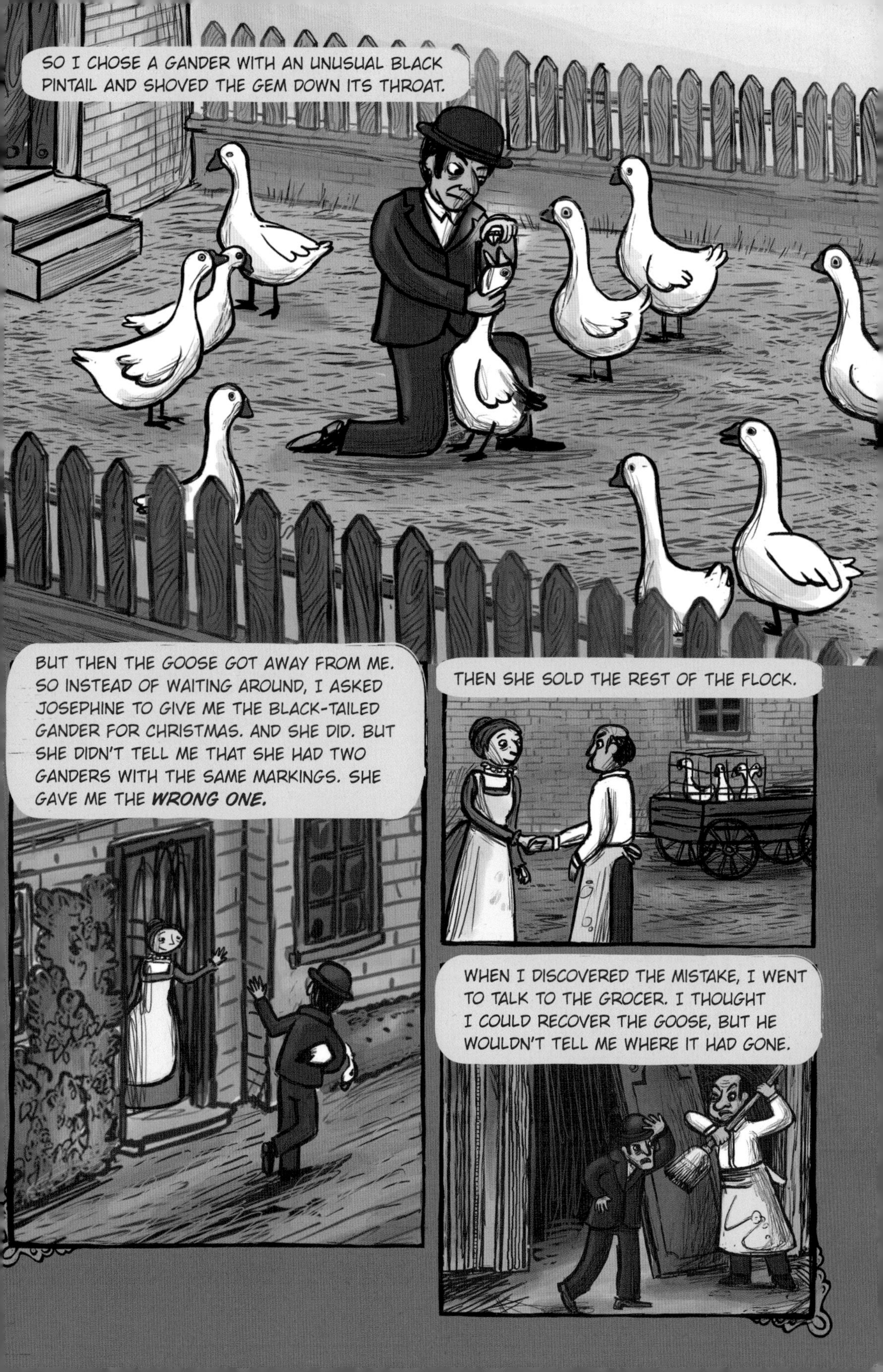
SO I CHOSE A GANDER WITH AN UNUSUAL BLACK PINTAIL AND SHOVED THE GEM DOWN ITS THROAT.
BUT THEN THE GOOSE GOT AWAY FROM ME. SO INSTEAD OF WAITING AROUND, I ASKED JOSEPHINE TO GIVE ME THE BLACK-TAILED GANDER FOR CHRISTMAS. AND SHE DID. BUT SHE DIDN'T TELL ME THAT SHE HAD TWO GANDERS WITH THE SAME MARKINGS. SHE GAVE ME THE ***WRONG ONE.***
THEN SHE SOLD THE REST OF THE FLOCK.
WHEN I DISCOVERED THE MISTAKE, I WENT TO TALK TO THE GROCER. I THOUGHT I COULD RECOVER THE GOOSE, BUT HE WOULDN'T TELL ME WHERE IT HAD GONE.

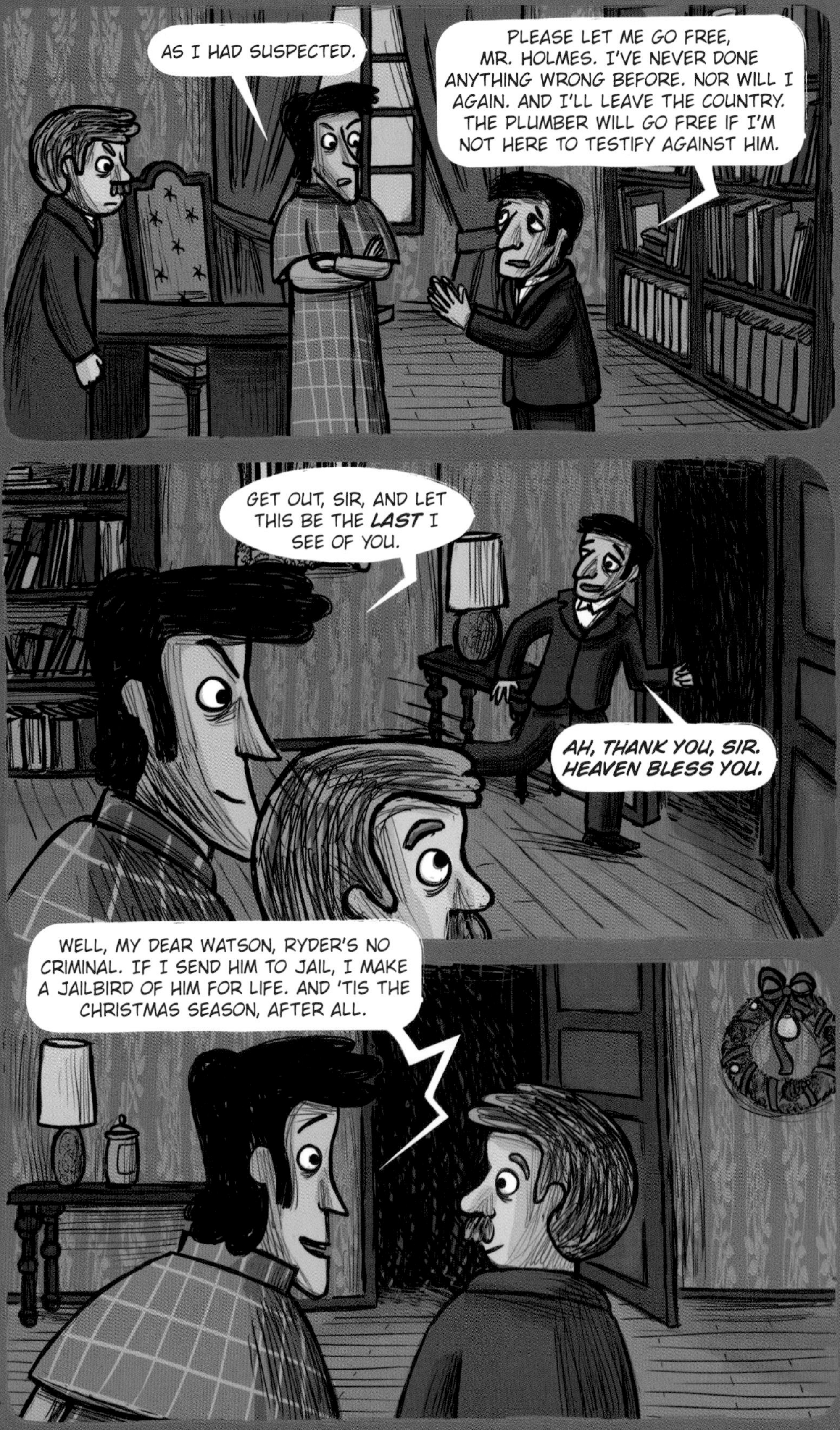
AS I HAD SUSPECTED.
PLEASE LET ME GO FREE, MR. HOLMES. I'VE NEVER DONE ANYTHING WRONG BEFORE. NOR WILL I AGAIN. AND I'LL LEAVE THE COUNTRY. THE PLUMBER WILL GO FREE IF I'M NOT HERE TO TESTIFY AGAINST HIM.
GET OUT, SIR, AND LET THIS BE THE *LAST* I SEE OF YOU.
AH, THANK YOU, SIR. HEAVEN BLESS YOU.
WELL, MY DEAR WATSON, RYDER'S NO CRIMINAL. IF I SEND HIM TO JAIL, I MAKE A JAILBIRD OF HIM FOR LIFE. AND 'TIS THE CHRISTMAS SEASON, AFTER ALL.

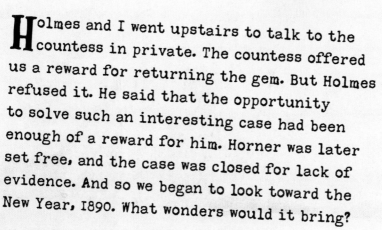

Holmes and I went upstairs to talk to the countess in private. The countess offered us a reward for returning the gem. But Holmes refused it. He said that the opportunity to solve such an interesting case had been enough of a reward for him. Horner was later set free, and the case was closed for lack of evidence. And so we began to look toward the New Year, 1890. What wonders would it bring?

From the Desk of
John H. Watson, M.D.

The Adventure of the Blue Gem: How Did Holmes Solve It?

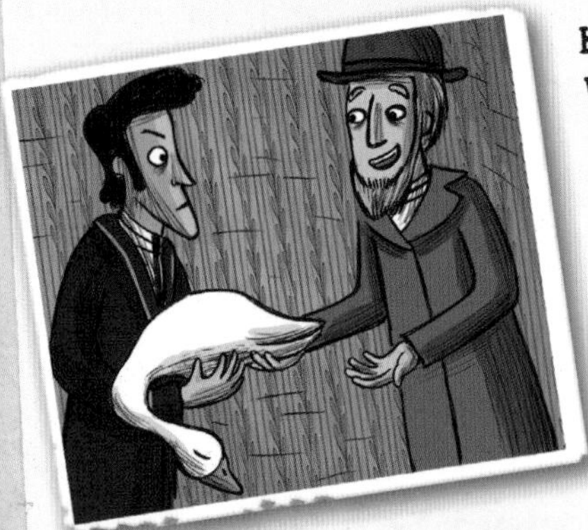

How did Holmes know that Henry Baker was innocent?

Since Henry Baker dropped the goose, Holmes figured that he had not been aware of the treasure he was carrying. This was confirmed when Baker accepted a new goose in exchange for the old one and didn't want the original goose's remaining parts.

How did Holmes know that Mr. Windigate was innocent?

Mr. Windigate of the Alpha Inn did not express interest in any specific goose or show any concern about Holmes's questions.

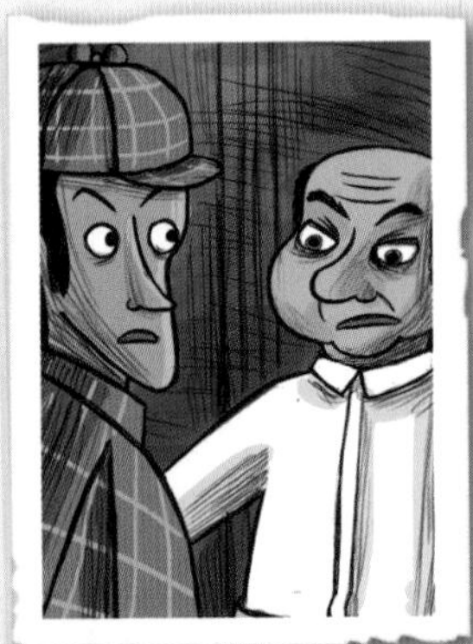

How did Holmes know that Mr. Breckinridge was innocent?

Breckinridge refused to tell Holmes where his geese had come from. So Holmes thought the grocer could have something to hide. He tested Breckinridge by using a wager to draw out information. If the man were guilty, a small bet would not have been enough to make him reveal the information Holmes needed.

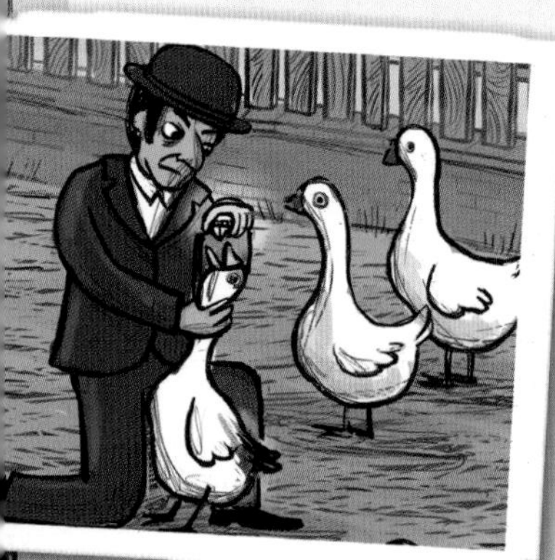

How did Holmes know James Ryder was the thief?

When Holmes saw a man arguing with Breckinridge about the black-tailed gander, Holmes suspected that this man was the thief. Holmes figured the man had lost the goose and was trying to get it back. So Holmes had to find out where and how the goose was lost. Then he would have enough evidence to catch the thief.

When Mrs. Oakshott told the story of the look-alike black-tailed ganders, Holmes suspected that her brother had placed the gem in the throat of one of the ganders and that she had given him the wrong one. This was confirmed by Ryder's confession.

Further Reading and Websites

Baliet, Blue. *Chasing Vermeer*. New York: Scholastic, 2005.

Baum, L. Frank. *A Christmas Treasury: Twelve Unforgettable Holiday Stories*. New York: Scholastic, 2000.

The Beacon Society
http://beaconsociety.com/Student.html

Bradley, James V. *The Canada Goose*. New York: Chelsea House, 2006.

Dickie, Lisa, and Ron Edwards. *Diamonds and Gemstones*. New York: Crabtree Publishing, 2004.

Gregory, Kristiana. *The Secret of the Junkyard Shadow*. New York: Scholastic, 2009.

Howard, Amanda. *Robbery File: The Museum Heist*. New York: Bearport Publishing, 2008.

Ibbotson, Eva. *The Secret Countess*. London: Young Picador, 2007.

Lawrence, Caroline. *The Man from Pomegranate Street*. London: Orion Children's Books, 2009.

Mineral and Gemstone Kingdom
http://www.minerals.net

MysteryNet.com Sherlock Holmes
http://www.mysterynet.com/holmes

Sherlock Holmes Museum
http://www.sherlock-holmes.co.uk

Trueit, Trudi Strain. *Rocks, Gems, and Minerals*. New York: Franklin Watts, 2003.

221 Baker Street
http://221bakerstreet.org

About the Author

Sir Arthur Conan Doyle was born on May 22, 1859. He became a doctor in 1882. When this career did not prove successful, Doyle started writing stories. In addition to the popular Sherlock Holmes short stories and novels, Doyle also wrote historical novels, romances, and plays.

About the Adapters

Murray Shaw's lifelong passion for Sherlock Holmes began when he was a child. He was the author of the Match Wits with Sherlock Holmes series published in the 1990s. For decades, he was a popular speaker in public schools and libraries on the adventures of Holmes and Watson.

M. J. Cosson is the author of more than fifty books, both fiction and nonfiction, for children and young adults. She has long been a fan of mysteries and especially of the great detective, Sherlock Holmes. In fact, she has participated in the production of several Sherlock Holmes plays. A native of Iowa, Cosson lives in the Texas Hill Country with her husband, dogs, and cat.

About the Illustrator

French artist Sophie Rohrbach began her career after graduating in display design at the Chambre des Commerce. She went on to design displays in many top department stores including Galeries Lafayette. She also studied illustration at Emile Cohl school in Lyon, France, where she now lives with her daughter. Rohrbach has illustrated many children's books. She is passionate about the colors and patterns that she uses in her illustrations.